Jacob Slater

I0683367

Out of
Control
The Zone 2
Bi-sexual Erotica

WARNING

This book contains sexually explicit scenes and adult language. It may be considered offensive to some readers. This book is for sale to adults ONLY.

* * * * * * * * * * * * * * * * * * *

Please store your files wisely where they cannot be accessed by underage readers.

Please feel free to send me an email. Just know that these emails are filtered by my publisher. Good news is always welcome.

Jacob Slater – **jacob_slater@awesomeauthors.org**

About the Publisher

4Fun Publishing, a member of **BLVNP Incorporated**, 340 S. Lemon #6200, Walnut CA 91789, info@blvnp.com / legal@blvnp.com
NOTE: Due to the highly emotional reaction of some people to works of erotic fiction, any email sent to the above address that contains foul language or religious references is automatically deleted by our anti-spam software and will not be seen. All other communications are welcome.

The Zone Series, Book 2

Out of Control
Bi-Sexual Erotica

By: Jacob Slater

© **Jacob Slater 2013**
ISBN: 978-1-62761-654-6

<u>Journal Entry #2</u>

Guayama, PR

It's been three days since we arrived at the compound. I was given my own room on the first floor. I find myself sitting at the mahogany desk next to the open window, a cool breeze blowing through my hair, where I look out at the rocky beach and the deep blue Caribbean waters that are lightly breaking on the sand. Any other time, I would have been happy to have a breathing, window-framed postcard that I could reach through with my hands, and if I wanted, walk out the door only a few feet from where I sit and begin to walk the short distance to the water. However, there will be no walk on the beach this morning. Not yet, at least.

The fact that I'm here at all has me almost numb, confused, and unsure if I am truly awake. Although I remember everything (including images that I would do anything to forget), I still feel as if none of this is real. Its questions and only questions that are in my mind now: Why am I here? What do they want? What should I do? I have no answers to these questions. So I sit and with the few pieces of paper that I was able to find in the small office next to the kitchen, I will attempt to get this jumbled mess of thoughts and memory out of my head and onto something real, something solid. The images are racing, and they move quickly, but I think I can do this.

I have talked little since arriving and the guards leave me to myself. Even with the door open, they will not enter my room; a rule that I am not aware of? The boy must be left alone? If so, why? What do they know? That doesn't matter. You do not want to remember. You are a coward. Stop it.

So I ignore them and they ignore me. It doesn't matter really, not at this point.

The pen is shaking in my hand. I am not scared, not anymore at least, but the pen wavers as I press the tip to the paper. Why? What does it know? What is it hiding? I should put the pen down. Yes, no reason to remember, to remember images and thoughts that do not stay in one place for long before I blink hard, shake my head, and they are gone. If I write, I will have no excuse, no reason to pretend that this is not real.

Has it been a week? I don't remember. Maybe it has been longer. The pen touched just a thread of the reality that has come unbundled and that is why my hand shakes. Maybe. I blink again, quickly, my eyes trying to block the memory. But no, I need to come back. I'm here again. I need to come back and remember...everything. My hand stops shaking. I begin to write now with purpose. I will remember.

It was a Sunday afternoon and my mother and I were returning home after a shopping trip to the mall. It had been a good day for the most part. My mother didn't get a chance to spend much time with me lately, as I was often running about with my friends. She enjoyed getting caught up on what was happening in my life. I had also had a pretty good day, as the car was now packed full of the new clothes that I would be taking with me when I headed off for college in just a few weeks. It was a good trade off. My mother heard about what movies I saw with my friends and I got clean underwear.

"So, you never did tell me about that fight you got into last week. Who was it with?" my mother asked, keeping her eyes on the road. She was acting as if she really didn't care, but was just checking. I knew better.

"Nobody you know," I answered quickly, trying to think of a way to change the conversation. My mother had noticed the red marks of my face the weekend before. I had lied and told her I had a fight with a friend. At the time she knew that I wasn't in the mood to talk about it, but evidently she had not forgotten and now she felt it was time she had a better explanation.

"Well, I don't like it," she said. "I didn't bring you up to get into fights. It's not like you."

"Mom, I really don't want to talk about it," I replied, not coming up with of anything that might get her off the subject.

After a pause, "I realize you're a young man now and I can't expect you to tell me everything, but I've been worried. You haven't been yourself this past week. You've been up in your room every night. You normally come down and spend some time with your dad and me, but you haven't all week." She wasn't going to let this drop.

"Mom, really, everything is fine. I just had a little problem last week but now everything is okay. Trust me. Everything is fine."

"It's a girl, isn't it?"

I had been sipping a soda and I choked a little, almost spilling the liquid on my shirt. "No mother, I can guarantee you it wasn't over a girl," I answered while wiping the spilled Pepsi from my chin and looking out the window so my mother couldn't see my eyes literally roll into the back of my head.

My mother continued to drive and I just kept my mouth shut. I knew she was still thinking about what might have happened to me last week, wondering what would cause me to hide away in my bedroom. I could tell her of course, but the thought of my parents knowing what happened sent a shiver down my spine. There was no way I was about to tell her anything close to the truth.

How do you tell your mother that not only are you gay, but also you enjoy getting fucked up the ass by big black men? Even if you send it with a gift, that story ain't going to play well with the folks. So I didn't say anything; I kept my eyes turned away and out the window. Eventually we were pulling onto the driveway and I sensed my ensuing escape, but it would not be a clean getaway.

"Well, if you want to talk about it, you let me know," my mother advised as I was climbing out of the car. "I'm not a boy but I remember how boys your age acted when I was your age. I know your hormones and juices and all that stuff gets in the way of your brain. So you just watch yourself, understand?"

I was not having a conversation about 'my juices and stuff' with my mother. "Thanks, Mom. I'll be fine. Trust me," I said as I quickly scooped up the packages in the backseat and walked quickly up the sidewalk and into the house.

"Well, you know where you can find me if you want to talk!" my mother yelled as I headed up the stairs and to my room. Yeah, I knew where she was and I wasn't going there. It had been a week and the piece of the phonebook with the telephone number written on it was still on my desk. I had looked at it every time I entered my room. I couldn't help it. My eyes were immediately drawn to it. The memory of what had happened the weekend before was still seared into my head and the piece of paper brought that memory back like a tidal wave every time I saw it.

I instinctively squeezed my ass cheeks thinking of the experience. I had been sore for the first couple of days but not nearly as much as I would have expected. That first night, before I went to bed, I wanted to feel my ass again to see how much it still hurt. I found some Vaseline in the bathroom and coated some on my middle finger.

Lying on my stomach, I reached between my cheeks and gently dabbed the jelly onto my ass and then slowly rubbed around my still bruised hole. It was sore all right, but it was neither stinging nor extremely painful. It was feeling more bruised than anything else. I kept rubbing around the circle and then slowly started to insert my finger until it was up to the first digit. With my finger now inside, I was able to feel around the rim of my ass. Again it was sore but not painful. I felt around a while, making sure everything was where it was supposed to be.

Suddenly, I noticed that I had a raging boner.

Closing my eyes, I again replayed the image of being pinned to a bed and having two huge black cocks practically rip open my hole. During the actual experience, my cock never got remotely hard but here I was, with my finger up my own ass, and it had never been harder. How weird is that? When I was having sex with those men, my cock didn't even come into the picture. But afterwards, there I was, thinking about it and my cock was rock solid.

I quickly rolled over and pulled my legs up to my chest, pretending that once again, I was preparing to take a huge, dark pole up my ass. I repositioned my finger at my hole and started to finger-fuck myself slowly at first and then faster. At the same time, I started to stroke my cock to the rhythm of my finger-fucking. Although it hurt a little because I was still sore, I closed my eyes and tried to mentally get back to where I was that afternoon.

The term that I had given to the mindset that I had achieved that afternoon was *The Zone*. I had used the same term before when I was working out. It was almost that same mental state when I was really hitting the weights hard or going that extra mile in a long run. It was the same, but it was different. When I was working out, getting in this *Zone* allowed me to do one more rep. When I was running, it allowed me to run just a little while longer than I might not have otherwise. When I was being fucked, getting in this *Zone* was different. Even though it allowed me to do things I otherwise might not have been able to do, it was more spiritual than physical. When I worked out or ran, it was just me. When I got fucked, there was someone else involved and they were pivotal in getting me in that state of mind where I thought I could do anything.

I stroked my cock faster and plunged my hole deeper with my fingers, trying to get into that state of mind again. Although I was physically enjoying the pleasure and sensation I was giving myself, it still wasn't nearly the same as the real fucking I had endured the weekend before. I felt my cock getting close to orgasm and I roughly squeezed another finger next to the first. It hurt a bit because I had not put on any additional Vaseline, but it was enough to put me over the top as my cock exploded and I shot a huge load. The first shot landed high on my chest and the remaining two or three shots landed squarely on my stomach. They did not dribble down the sides of my stomach as they usually did. I pulled out my fingers, went to the bathroom, cleaned up, and went to bed.

It had been a week since the encounter with the two strangers and I had not picked up the phone. I had spent a lot of time thinking about what had happened and why I had allowed it to happen. Alone in my room I played the scene over and over again in my head. Why did I do it? Why did I let this guy take me back to his place and do those things to me? More importantly, why did I enjoy it so much? They were questions that had no answer and it would no doubt, be some time before I came to terms with who I was and what I was becoming.

Several times, I picked up the phone and was in the middle of dialing the number only to chicken-out and hang up. Was I fucking nuts? Was I really going to call this guy and let him pimp out my ass to strangers so he could make money? That was fucking ridiculous!

Now, that a week had passed, the memory was starting to fade a bit into something closer to a dream. I knew it happened. There was no question about that. But I was starting to mark it off as just a strange experience, an adventure that would not be duplicated.

"Really," I thought. "What in the hell was I thinking?"

I finally got up the nerve and took the phone number and got rid of it. I not only got rid of it, I burned it on the stove so that there would be no way for me to change my mind later. I knew that my "juices and stuff" might try and trick me so I was taking no chances. This number was getting trashed and I was moving on with my life. End of story.

It was Sunday afternoon. It had been a week and a day since the encounter. I was getting ready to head out of the house and go meet a friend and see a movie. I had cleared my head of all the thoughts about what had happened and I was going to go be a *normal* kid again. Yes sir, that is exactly what I was going to do...until I walked out the front door and saw Martin sitting in his car that was now parked right in front of my house.

I stopped, frozen in my tracks. *This is not happening*, I thought. The man who had practically raped me was not sitting in front of my house in his car smoking a cigarette. But he was.

I turned around and saw my mother in the kitchen window. She wasn't looking out, occupied with preparing something on the countertop, but at any moment she could just turn around and see this guy parked in front of our house. I knew my mother and she would not waste any time before investigating. The houses in our neighborhood were big and spread apart; no one just came and parked in front of one of them without having a reason. She would come out and ask him what he was doing.

Oh my God, I was in deep shit. I looked at the car, then my mother, then the car, then my mother, and back and forth several times before I started to get a hold of my senses. I had to do something, and do it quick.

I casually walked up to his car window and bent down, appearing to act as if one of my shoes were untied. Without looking up I played with my shoelaces and whispered, "What are you doing here? You have to leave now or I will get in trouble. Please, just leave."

"Hey there Little Man. I've been waiting for the phone to ring, but it be silent so far. What's up with that?" Martin said casually. I looked up from my shoes and watched as he inhaled on his cigarette, leaned back in his seat, and blew a smoke ring across his steering wheel. He wasn't going anywhere.

"I've been watching that fine woman in there. That be your mother, Little Man? Yes indeed, she is mighty fine. I bet your papa is one happy man. Am I right? I say, am I right?"

"Martin, please, you really have to go," I urged, still kneeling down. "If my mother comes out here I will be in so much trouble, and so will you. Please, I beg you, just go."

Still staring ahead, Martin did not appear to hear a word I had said. "Why haven't you called me, boy? I thought you and me had ourselves a little deal. You do know what day it is, don't you?"

I didn't reply.

"Well let me remind you, Little Man. It be Sunday. More importantly, it be more than a week since we had our..." he hesitated a couple of seconds, "...our little ren-dez-vous." He punctuated every syllable as if pleased that he had thought of such a big word. My initial plan of begging and pleading for him to just get the hell out of here was going nowhere fast.

"What do you want?" I asked urgently, looking back again to see that my mother was thankfully still preoccupied with her cooking. "We can talk about this somewhere else. Please just pull up around the corner and we can talk." Anger had started to set in. Who did he think he was? How dare he try to scare me when he was the one who should be afraid. If my mother found out what he had done she would call the cops and although I would have a lot of explaining to do, he would go to jail.

I had had enough with this thug and I was taking charge. I stood up and started to walk down the sidewalk. If he wanted to talk, then he was going to have to follow me to the corner.

Martin honked the horn.

"I'm dead," I mumbled to myself, pressing one hand against my forehead.

I looked back at the car, and then at my house. I could no longer see my mother from the window and she was no doubt heading to the front door to find out what was going on. I walked to Martin's window and leaned my head in. "Martin, my mother is coming. If you ever want to see me again, for any reason, I suggest you leave."

"Well, Little Man, I'll make a deal with you," he said, flicking his spent cigarette out the window and onto the street. "You meet me at the park this afternoon at five, near the bathroom where we first had our little encounter. If you don't show up I will be placing this here picture somewhere near where that pretty mama of yours can find it." He then reached into his glove compartment and pulled out a Polaroid photo. It was of his roommate Jake on top of me, with my legs pinned to the bed, and his massive cock crammed completely up my ass.

Oh my god, when the fuck did he take a picture without me knowing? I didn't have a chance to think about that question before I heard the front door open. Glancing over my shoulder I saw my mother, now looking quite serious, starting to walk across the yard to where Martin and I now stood.

"Five o'clock, Little Man," said Martin. He then started his car, put it in drive, and slowly just drove away, leaving me standing in the road and looking at my mother, who was now standing on the sidewalk with her hands on her hips.

"Who was that?"

Think fast, Little Man.

"I don't know. He was asking how to get to Wrigley Field."

"He was looking for Wrigley Field my ass. What are you up to, young man?"

First I was *Little Man* and now I was *Young Man*.

"Really, he just asked how to get to Wrigley Field," I asserted, trying to act as if her assumption of me not telling the truth was absurd.

"Do you think I'm stupid? Is that it?" she responded.

"No," I replied, not sure where she was going with this.

"I saw what he pulled out of the glove box, young man," she continued. "I'm not like all your little friends' mothers. I pay attention to my kid's life and I know when something is up, and something is definitely up."

Feeling hopelessly caught, I decided to not even try to play the game anymore. I had lost and she had won.

"Okay, he wasn't looking for Wrigley Field." Although I would not lie to her anymore, I wasn't about to just spill the entire can of beans either.

"What was it? Pot? Cocaine? What was he trying to sell you?" she asked.

"Huh?"

"He was trying to sell you drugs, wasn't he?" she asked.

Maybe I wasn't so busted after all.

My mother, bless her heart, has always lived a very comfortable, yet isolated life. Like my father, she had grown up with money, attended private schools, and for the most part only associated with people just like herself: that being mostly rich and very, very white. She wasn't a snob exactly, but someone who hadn't experienced the salad bowl of colors and cultures that made up the world.

Unfortunately when one is so secluded and protected from the real world, they tend to make their assumptions about how the *other people* live from sources other than reality. In my mother's case, that would be the television. Not being someone who had any interest in situation comedies, she would often gravitate to the myriad of cop and detective dramas that flood the airways. An unfortunate byproduct of such selective viewing is that one gets the assumption that every Black, Hispanic, and Puerto Rican man was either a drug user or a drug dealer. Just as the rest of the world watches American television and believes that the majority of Americans live in 10 bedroom mansions, with a swimming pool, and a maid, and dance to Britney Spears' music, my mother believed that except for Bill Cosby, there was no such thing as a black man who didn't have a desire to get the world hooked on drugs.

One time at a drive-thru restaurant, my mother was reaching out the window to pay the Latino teenager manning the cash register when the young man asked my mother if she had a dime. "I don't think so young man," she responded harshly. "And you had better hope that by the time I get home I don't call the police." The cashier, looking surprised, handed her the change and we drove off.

"What was that all about?" I asked.

"Didn't you hear him? He asked me if I had..." she hesitated, trying to find the right word "...some Mary Jane."

"What are you talking about?" I asked, amazed.

"A dime bag, stupid! Weren't you listing?"

"Mother," I replied, beginning to rub my temples. "The food was seven dollars and ten cents. You handed him a ten-dollar bill. He asked if you had a dime so he could just give you three dollars instead of a bunch of change."

"You think so, Mr. Smarty Pants. Shows what you know. One of these days me and you are going to take a drive to South Chicago and I am going to show you exactly how these people live. Change my ass."

Why a complete stranger would assume my mother had a "dime bag" on her did not occur to her. There was no arguing with her knowledge of how the world worked and I didn't try. I imagine her meeting Collin Powell one day and although honored to meet him I can picture her scanning his pockets with her eyes looking for the eight ball of coke surely hidden somewhere in his military jacket.

I lifted my head and looked at her where she was still standing on the sidewalk, waiting for an explanation.

"Okay, he wanted to know if I wanted to buy some..." I hesitated, trying to think what my mother would find truthful, "...weed."

She continued to stare me down with her eyes, not blinking, trying to see if I would snap. It almost worked before she responded, "Well...that son-of-a-bitch is damn lucky I didn't get his license plate number. I mean, really, does that guy think anyone around here would want to buy any of his weed?"

"You scared him off, mom. Good job." I tried to sound thankful that she had arrived just in time to save me from this stranger who surely wanted no less than to see me completely drugged out of my mind before the age of twenty.

"If he comes around here again, just stay away from him and come get me. You got that?"

She started walking back into the house, stopped, then turned around. "One more thing. If I see you do something so stupid as to go up to a complete stranger's car again I will shove the heel of my shoe so far up your ass that it will take you days to dig it out." She turned around and walked back to the house and went inside, firmly closing the door behind her.

After Martin left I headed to my room to think. My mother was in the kitchen and thankfully left me alone for the remainder of the afternoon. As I was lying in bed I wondered how he had managed to take a picture of me getting fucked by his roommate without me realizing it. He must have come in the room when Jake was really fucking me hard because I didn't remember hearing or seeing any flash. Also, how did he know where I lived? The photo was at least somewhat explainable, but how did he get my address?

Given the circumstances, I had no choice but to meet him. After his little display in front of my house I had no doubt that Martin would not hesitate to follow through on his threat. He had shown that he didn't care what problems he might cause, and since I was heading off to college in a couple of months I could not let anything jeopardize my plans. I'm not sure what my parents would do if they saw that photo. They would probably assume that I was raped or forced into doing those things, but if confronted I don't believe that I could actually lie. The truth would eventually come out.

They would know that I willingly went to a strange man's apartment for sex and once that truth was out I wasn't sure how my family would react. For all I knew they would cut me off completely. Although at 18 I was desperate for freedom and couldn't wait to get out of my parents' house, I was not quite so willing to have that freedom without the financial benefits that my parents would no doubt be providing me. If my parents cut me off financially I wouldn't know what to do. I've never known what it was like not being taken care of financially.

No, I had to go meet Martin and find out what he wanted.

I headed out around 4:00 telling my Mother I was going over to friend's house nearby. Surprisingly, she did not ask for details, only to "be sure and be home by ten or call if you are going to be late." After walking a few blocks I hailed a cab and within 15 minutes I was being dropped off in the parking lot at the park. I paid the driver, and then headed into the park and towards the bathroom where this whole crazy experience started.

I was beginning to get a little nervous as I approached the bathroom, but as I came closer I saw that Martin was nowhere to be found. I went inside and found no one. After searching the area I decided to wait and sit under a tree near the restroom where I would have a good view of the surroundings.

I sat there about 30 minutes and watched several men use the restroom. Although I couldn't tell for sure, it looked like most were using the facilities for their intended purpose, however a couple of older men tended to hang around just a little too long and appeared to be cruising the place.

No one hung around for more than a couple of minutes and it made me think that fate must have thrown me a curve ball for me to have come to this particular bathroom at exactly the same time Martin had been in there. I wondered why he had been in there and whether he was cruising or was he just using the place to take a piss. I guess it didn't make a hell of a lot of difference at this point.

It was getting close to 5:00 and I was starting to get nervous again. I didn't have a clue why Martin was doing this or what he wanted. When I had met him last week, he had made it appear that I had a choice as to whether to hook up with him again or not. I obviously had decided that I didn't want to do anything like that again, but evidently that was not the decision that Martin wanted to hear. I assumed that he took the picture as insurance in case I didn't call. But then again, he took the picture before we had any discussions about me calling him and "working" for him in the first place. It just didn't make sense.

I was thinking about these things when I noticed a Latino kid about my age walk into the bathroom. He was wearing the typical baggy pants that were 2 sizes too big and a white tank top shirt that showed his skinny, yet muscular body. His head was shaved and although his skin was dark, it was not nearly as dark as most of the other Latino guys that I went to school with.

He went into the bathroom and came out within a few seconds. He obviously did not have to use the bathroom, as he was not in there long enough to do his business. He walked around the small building and then started to gaze around at the park as if he was looking for someone. Finally, he happened to glance in my direction and without any hesitation started to walk toward where I was sitting. I was a little surprised that he was heading towards me, but I didn't give it much thought, as my mind was still preoccupied with what was going to happen when Martin showed up.

He came to where I was sitting and asked, "Are you waiting for Martin?"

I was expecting him to ask me for a cigarette or maybe a couple of bucks, but I didn't expect this. I was a little stunned as I responded, "Yeah."

"He asked me to come here and get you. We need to head back to his place. Let's go." He then turned around and started to walk away.

I quickly got up and started to follow him as my mind raced with questions. Who was this kid? How many people knew about this? What in the hell was going on?

"Hey, just a second. Wait up!" I called after him.

He stopped and turned around, looking at me. When he did I was able to get a better look of this new stranger. He was about my height and probably weighed around 150 pounds. He looked much more muscular up close and not quite as skinny as he did just before. He had a little goatee, but there was not much hair and it was very thin. I noticed that his skin was very smooth and appeared to be completely hairless. Upon closer inspection he was actually quite handsome.

"Who are you? Where's Martin?" I asked.

"He's back at his place getting things ready. He didn't have time to come out here and get your ass, so he asked me to do it for him."

He didn't tell me his name and I didn't pressure him any further as he appeared to be a little upset, although I had no idea as to why.

"Well, can you at least tell me what's going on? Martin asked me to meet him here and that's all I know. I wouldn't even be here, but Martin..." I stopped, not quite ready to tell him the entire story.

"I've seen the picture man, so don't worry about it. Let's go and I'll explain in the car." He then turned and started walking towards the parking lot again.

After hesitating, I quickly followed and soon enough we came upon Martin's familiar beat up junker sitting in the parking lot. The kid unlocked the car, climbed in, and then reached over and unlocked my side of the door. Once again I was getting into Martin's car at the park and getting ready to head over to his place. Just like Martin had done the week earlier the kid opened a pack of cigarettes, lit one up, started the car, and headed out of the parking lot toward Martin's apartment.

As we drove away he didn't say a word and didn't explain any further about what was going on. I couldn't stand it anymore. My nerves had all they could take and I was getting to the end of my patience.

"You said you would explain in the car what in the hell was going on, so tell me. All I know is that Martin picked me up last week, took me back to his apartment where both he and his roommate royally fucked the shit out of me, and then this afternoon he shows up at my house demanding that I be at the park at five o'clock. So please, tell me just what in the fuck is going on!"

All the stress of the situation was finally coming to a head; I was shaking and almost in tears. I had had all I could take and was losing it fast.

"Man, just calm down," he said as he glanced at me nervously. "No one is fucking with you, so just calm down."

"Then tell me just what the fuck is going on," I demanded, still quite upset but starting to get a little under control again. "And who are you anyway?"

"The name is Arturo. Nice to meet you." He put his cigarette in his mouth and reached over with his right hand to grasp my trembling hand. "Don't be freaking on me or anything. I don't need the hassle. Just calm your ass down and everything is going to be fine. You got that?"

I nodded in agreement. At least he was talking now.

"I know why you are here. Martin told me, so no need to worry about any of that shit. I don't want to get into any particulars, but Martin kind'a did the same to me so I know how you are feeling about now. All you need to know is that everything is cool."

"Martin took a picture of you too?" I asked, stunned.

"Like I said, I don't want to get into any particulars. Let's just say I don't want to be here anymore than you do, but there is no way around that right now, so you might as well get used to it."

This was getting stranger by the moment. Apparently I was not the only one who had been tricked by Martin. He had evidently tricked this kid as well, although he wasn't supplying any details.

Since he was talking I decided I would at least try to get some additional information out of him.

"So, what is going on this afternoon? Why are we going to Martin's place?"

Arturo continued to drive for a few moments apparently ignoring my question, before replying, "We need to do a little work." He took another long drag off his cigarette before blowing it toward the windshield. "Martin has these parties for special friends of his, and he likes to supply them with whatever they want. Usually all they want is to get fucked up, smoke some shit, do some lines, whatever. Most of them like to fuck some pussy." He took another drag on his cigarette, his face looking like he was thinking about something serious, before continuing more softly. "Some of his buddies don't want no pussy."

I didn't get a chance to think about what he meant by that because he was already starting to turn into the apartment's driveway and pulling around toward the back parking lot. I didn't say a word and just stared at Arturo and wondered what in the hell I had gotten myself into. I was desperately trying to figure a way out of this situation, but nothing was coming to mind. I was in this for the entire ride and I started to realize that when Arturo parked the car and got out.

I got out of the car and followed him to the stairway that I had emerged from a week earlier. I followed behind him, carefully walking down the stairs, but instead of going to the door where I had gone last time he turned and knocked on the door that was at the opposite side of the landing. After a couple of seconds I heard the lock being turned and the door opened and Jake appeared, standing in the doorway smiling. He wasn't wearing the shabby clothes that he wore the last time we had met. He had cleaned up rather well. He was clean-shaven, his hair slicked back, and he had on a pair of black slacks with a white silk shirt.

"Well, well, look who decided to come and pay us a visit. Come on in boys, come on in." He then stood aside as I followed Arturo into the apartment.

Although I was extremely nervous and a little scared, part of me was beginning to give in to the realization that there were circumstances taking place that were now very much outside my control. The only thing I could do now was to stay alert and just try and figure out exactly what was happening and see if there was any way I could somehow undo this mess that I had gotten myself into.

After walking through the doorway, Jake closed and locked the door behind me. As my eyes adjusted to the dim light in the room I noticed that we were once again not alone. There were several women dressed in what my father called "slut wear" who were standing around a small bar that had been built into the corner of the living room. As I looked around I also noticed that unlike the other apartment, this one was bigger and much nicer. There was the bar area that had stools and a stocked liquor cabinet. There was a den area that had a big screen TV, a huge stereo system, and a fireplace. The walls had real wood paneling, which gave the room a cabin-like feeling. There was a kitchen that I could see through a cut out in the wall next to the bar. There was a hallway that led off from the bar, but I could not see where it went.

As I looked around the room I was startled when Jake grabbed my arm. "Let me show you around before the party starts." He then led me toward the bar. "Do you want anything to drink? Now is your chance, because later you won't have nothin' for a while."

I didn't understand what he was talking about, but replied, "I'll have a coke."

"Anything in it? Rum? Whiskey?" he asked, being extremely polite.

"No, thanks. I don't drink."

"Suit yourself," Jake responded as he reached into the built-in refrigerator and pulled out a can of Coke, opened it, and gave it to me.

I took it from him and noticed that Arturo was fixing himself a tall drink from the bar. I couldn't tell what he was making, but it sure wasn't a soft drink.

Jake then walked past the women at the bar, not paying them any notice, and turned into the hallway. I looked back and Arturo was staying at the bar with his drink. As I turned back to follow Jake he was heading all the way to the end of the hallway, passing several closed doors. One went to the kitchen, but that was all I could see. What were behind the other doors were unknown to me. When I got to the end of the hall, Jake reached forward and opened the door and led me inside.

"This is where you will be staying for the evening," he said as I walked past him into the room. I walked through the doorway and Jake flipped on the light switch.

My first impression was that I had walked onto some strange movie set. I had expected a bedroom, and indeed it was, but this was no ordinary bedroom.

The first thing I noticed was that there were mirrors on every wall; they ran from floor to ceiling. There were no windows, no pictures, nothing except for the mirrors. There was a single light bulb that hung from the ceiling. There were no other lights in the room. In the middle of the room there was a large king-sized bed. It was not against the wall, but in the very middle of the room. It did not have a headboard and there was just a black fitted sheet covering the mattress. In one corner of the room there was a small table with some items on top of it which I could not identify. Other than the table and the bed, there was nothing in the room.

I stood there not moving, amazed, my mind racing with what it was being presented with.

"So what's you think?" asked Jake, as he shut the door and proceeded to go and sit on the bed. He patted the bed with his hand, gesturing me to come and sit next to him.

I didn't move. I couldn't move. I was too stunned.

"I ain't gonna bite. Come on over here 'cause you and me need to have a little talk."

Slowly, as if in a daze, I came and sat down next to Jake on the bed, while continuing to glance around the room. It was too much and my brain just wasn't working at full speed at the moment.

"This be where you are gonna work tonight," Jake said, putting his arm around my shoulder. "Don't worry. You ain't going to be alone. Art will be right here with you the entire time to show you the ropes."

"What...what do you mean work?" I asked.

Jake just looked at me as if I was the dumbest person on the face of the earth. "Ain't you figured it out, boy?" he said while tapping his finger against my forehead. "Martin and I run us a little business. You don't need to know the details of what that business is, but part if it involves letting our business partners have a little fun once in a while. We have ourselves a little party, see, and we let the boys have their fun. Whatever they want, we give it to them. You understand that, boy?" he asked, lightly slapping my face a couple of times to make sure that I was hearing what he was saying.

I didn't understand anything. I wasn't even close to understanding anything; I was too stunned to think anymore. All I could do was shake my head from side to side.

Jake took a big breath, sighed, and continued, "In a little bit some friends, or should I say partners, of ours are going to come over for some business. After we get done we like to celebrate with a little party. That's where you and the girls come in. The girls go in a couple of the rooms and you and Art come in here. If someone want to party with the girls, then we supply the pussy. If they want to party with the boys, then we give them some ass. You understandin' now, boy?"

Slowly, it started to make sense to me. Martin and Jake were going to give me up to their friends to use as they wish. I was going to get used by people I had never met before. I was sitting in a room designed purely for sex and I was going to be one of the major players. Yes indeed, I understood now.

"Just relax. No one is coming for a while. Take a nap or somethin'." Jake then got up, walked to the door, opened it and left, closing the door behind him and leaving me alone to think about the predicament I was in.

I sat there for a couple of minutes and did nothing. I didn't even drink my coke. *This was not happening.* I was not sitting in a room waiting for any strange man to come in and have sex with me. How had all this happened?

I was sitting in my stupor when the door opened and Martin walked in and shut the door behind him.

"Hey there Little Man, nice that you could make it."

He came over and stood in front of me, while I said nothing and just stared up at him. He was smiling down at me, with a smirk on his face. He reached down and lightly grabbed my chin and guided my face up to meet his own.

"Let's me and you get something straight right now. You belong to me and you'll do anything I ask. You got that, boy?" He didn't raise his voice, and talked as if he really cared about me.

"Why are you doing this?" I asked softly, looking at him and hoping that he would just let me leave.

"What do you mean 'why am I doing this?' You asked me to, boy. Don't you remember?" He continued to stare down at me with an expression of mild bewilderment and surprise.

The frustration that had been building in me all day had given me a little courage and I didn't feel like taking any more of this guy's shit. I had had enough and I wasn't interested in being nice anymore.

"What do you mean I asked for it?" I said sarcastically, beginning to raise my voice. "I didn't ask to come here. I wouldn't be here except for that picture and that little stunt you pulled in front of my house. I don't know what the fuck you're talking about."

Still smiling Martin said, "Well, maybe you just have a bad memory. Let me see if I can help you out."

With that, he suddenly reached forward and grabbed my hair, pulling me off the bed. I was startled and tried to struggle, but the pain of him pulling on my hair brought some sense into me and I stopped struggling immediately.

"Lay the fuck down on the bed, face down," he demanded, now angrily, his voice tense. He then shoved me forward onto the bed and I fell forward. I quickly rolled over onto my stomach and hid my face, expecting that he might try and punch me. Within a second his weight was once again on top of me, pressing me down into the familiar position when he had first taken me. This time though, we both had our clothes on. He moved his hands underneath my arms and once again had them clamped around my neck, pinning me to the bed, leaving me helpless.

"Please, what are you doing?" I begged, scared. All courage that I previously had was now gone.

"What am I doing? I'm helping that poor memory of yours, you little fuck head! Now you fucking just think for a second. Try and remember what happened last week and what agreement we made." He was now almost yelling and I had no doubt that if anyone was within 20 feet of the door they would be able to hear him. I didn't think anyone was going to come and help me.

He continued, his voice getting even louder, "Now you tell me exactly what you said to me last week when I had you pinned down like this. Just what in the fuck were your exact words to me after I shoved my cock up your fucking little white ass? Tell me, motherfucker!"

"I don't know what you're talking about," I whimpered.

"I gave you a fucking choice last week. You do remember that don't you, fucker?"

My thoughts were only of trying to get out of this room. I couldn't remember anything about last week. I was too terrified.

"I'm sorry," I whimpered, "I don't remember." I started to cry and the tears rolled freely down my face.

"Take a deep breath, and just think for a second. I know that little brain of yours will remember if you just fucking think."

Martin was now calming down somewhat, but he still was still pinning me quite hard to the bed. "Think Little Man, what choice did I give you last week?"

A choice? What in the hell was he talking about?

And then I remembered.

I suddenly remembered every single word that we exchanged. The memory came back as if it had just taken place. He indeed had given me a choice. That choice was to get up and leave the first time I had been with him. He had made it plain and simple. At the time I had thought that he was just being nice, but evidently his offer was more serious than I had the ability to understand.

"I remember," I said quietly, letting my face slowly press flat against the bed.

The choice I was given was that I could either leave, or see what I was made of and take whatever he had to give. I remembered now as if it had just happened all over again. With his weight again pressing down on my body and his arms pinning me again to the bed, I began to remember what thoughts were going through my head a week earlier. I remembered the decision and I remember what I told him.

Martin now leaned forward and whispered in my ear, "You remember now Little Man? Tell me again, what exactly did you tell me last week when I gave your fucking pussy ass a chance to get the fuck up and get out. Just exactly what did you tell me? Tell me what you said. Come on, tell me."

He had me and he knew it. I used to think I was a smart kid. I thought I was always one step ahead of everyone else. Now here I was the last one to figure it all out.

Once again I found myself slowly turning my head as I had done a week earlier, and looking back at the man who was on top of me, controlling me, using me.

"I said, 'Please sir, please make me your bitch.'"

A smile broke out on Martin's face then. He slowly nodded his head and said, "Well, well, well. My Little Man has finally figured it out. I'm proud of you boy, I really am."

He then let go of my arms and neck, rolled off me, and stood up. I rolled over onto my side to look at him starring down at me.

"Now, get out of your fucking clothes, bitch, and you do whatever any motherfucker who walks in here wants you to do tonight. You got that?"

"Yes sir." I replied, not looking at him in the face, ashamed.

"You do as you're told and maybe me and you can work out a little agreement where you will have a little more choice in when you come and work for me. Until then, you do whatever the fuck I tell you to, understand?"

"Yes, sir."

"And one more thing," he reached inside his pocket and pulled out a plastic card that I couldn't quite make out, and threw it on the bed. "I think you forgot this the last time you were here." He then turned around and walked out of the room and shut the door.

I didn't move for a while and finally looked down to see what he had thrown on the bed. I picked it up and brought it closer so I could take a look.

Of course. It all made sense now. I was holding my own student identification card. It had my picture, my address, and my home phone number printed right on it. It must have fallen out of my shorts when I had taken them off last week. Either that or Martin had searched my pockets. At least now I knew how he had found out where I lived. I took the ID and shoved it deep into my pants. My own fucking student ID. I was so stupid.

I slowly stood up and began to get undressed.

~oOo~

I was nervous. I wouldn't exactly say I was scared, but I was definitely very, very nervous. Here I was, sitting on a bed, in my underwear, in a bizarre bedroom that looked like it was designed for a cheap porn shoot. What made it worse is that I could see exactly how I looked. In the mirrors plastering the walls I saw a scared kid that at one time used to be confident, even cocky, but now was barely holding on to what little self-respect he had left. I kept running my fingers through my hair nervously, taking deep breaths, and trying to sort it all out.

I was by myself for about 10 minutes when the door opened. I was startled, but relaxed when I saw that it was Arturo. He came in with a drink still in hand, ignoring me, and walked over to the only table in the room. I didn't say anything as he opened the drawer under the table and pulled out a small hand mirror and set it on the table. He reached into his pocket and pulled out a small, folded piece of paper. He carefully opened the packet and I could see what at first looked like white powder. I thought it was cocaine, which I had seen a couple of times before at parties, but when he scattered some of the contents onto the mirror I could see that it was not a powder but more like tiny, clear pebbles, or crystals.

He poured a few of these crystals on the mirror, refolded the paper, and put it back in his pocket. He then reached into his other pocket and pulled out a small pocketknife. He flipped open one of the blades and then proceeded to carefully chop the crystals. There was a look of concentration on his face as he chipped away, then scooped the now more finer particles into a pile, chopped again with his knife, then repeated the process over and over. His eyes never left the mirror and it was clear he had done this many times.

After a couple of minutes leaning over the mirror and going through this repetitive process he finally stood up, carefully licked the edges of the blade, folded it, and put the pocket knife back in his pants. He then reached into his back pocket and pulled out what looked like a small, clear straw but as I looked closer I saw that it was a hollow plastic ballpoint pen that had the insides removed. He then leaned over the desk where he had just formed several lines of the unknown powder on the mirror.

Taking the hollowed out pen he then proceeded to put one end to his nose, leaned all the way over the table, placed a finger over his left nostril, and then starting at one end of the lines began to inhale, moving the pen as he did. The line of powder disappeared as the plastic tube approached, as if picked up by a vacuum hose, and disappeared into his right nostril. He stood up, leaned his head back, and quickly pinched and tugged on his nose several times with his left thumb and forefinger as he continued to inhale.

With his other hand still holding the plastic tube he held it out to me, acknowledging my presence for the first time since he entered the room. "Want some?"

"No, no thanks," I replied as he began to walk toward me.

I had originally thought the stuff was coke but the color was not white like I had seen the few times before. I knew coke was not as harmful as most adults would like you to believe but I had no idea what this stuff was so I decided I would pass. I also didn't want to find myself not only kept in a room to do unknown things while at the same time being completely fucked up. It wasn't worth the risk, I quickly determined.

"So you ready for a pajama party or something?" Arturo asked, looking at me up and down. I wasn't sure if he was trying to make a joke, or trying to make me uncomfortable as I stood there in my underwear. Neither one of us laughed and I became very aware that I was standing in his presence almost completely nude.

"Martin told me to get undressed," I said, feeling even more embarrassed as he continued to stare at me.

Arturo suddenly turned and tossed himself on the bed, rolled over on his back, looked at the ceiling and began to take several large and deep breaths. He also began to run his fingers across the top of his head as if he were running them through his hair. With his head shaved though it looked a little odd and I wondered if he was feeling some of the effects of whatever he had just put up his nose.

Laying back on the bed and talking to the ceiling, he advised me, "The guys just showed up a couple of minutes ago. They won't be ready to party for a while. They've got to finish their business first." He continued to rub his head with his hands.

Although I hadn't asked for an update of what was happening in the other room I was appreciative that he felt some obligation to keep me informed. "What business is that?" I asked, turning to face him on the bed.

"Best if you don't know. I don't know all of it myself, but I know when to mind my own business." He then suddenly sat up and pulled out a pack of cigarettes from his pocket and lit one up. He took a deep drag on the cigarette and then asked, "So, you a fag or something?"

The bluntness of his questions caught me off guard, but I didn't see any reason to try and bullshit him. "Yeah, I'm gay. What about you?"

"No fucking way, man. I don't like none of this shit," he said as he slowly shook his head from side to side.

"Then why are you here?" I couldn't begin to think why he was here if he wasn't somehow being coerced like me. I at least got myself into this predicament because I was gay to begin with and had gotten in over my head. I wondered if he was somehow being coerced in some other way by Martin, or possibly Jake.

He continued to smoke his cigarette for a while before responding, "It ain't no business but my own."

I knew when to keep my mouth shut, so I did. We looked at each other in silence for a while before Arturo once again got up and went over to the table. There was an ashtray on the table where he put out his cigarette. He then proceeded to inhale two more lines from the mirror. He again went through the motions of standing up, sniffing, and pulling on his nose.

I was getting up the nerve to ask Arturo additional questions to determine why he was here when the door opened and Jake came in, shutting the door behind him.

"I just wanted to make sure you boys are doing okay in here and weren't getting into any trouble," he said, smiling. If you didn't know any better he could easily have just been sticking his head in a room to check on his kids. He then walked over to where I was sitting and reached down with his hand to caress my face. Any similarities at that point vanished. "Man, you sure are one fine white boy. You know I'll be having some more of you tonight," he said, more talking to himself than me. He then looked over at Arturo, the smile leaving his face. "And you! Get outta them clothes before Martin comes in here. You know he want you to be ready when the party be startin'."

"Whatever you say. You're the boss," came Arturo's reply as he looked at Jake with contempt.

Jake looked at Arturo with a hard stare before responding quietly but firmly. "Don't get smart with me, boy. You don't want to piss me off." He then returned his attention to me, acting as if no one else was in the room. His smile returned and he continued to rub the side of my face with his hand, and then taking his fingers and rubbing them on my lips. "Boy, you sure are pretty. Damn pretty. I may not be able to wait until later to get some of you." He then reached down with his other hand and started to unbuckle his pants. "Why don't you get down here boy and suck daddy's cock for a little bit."

I didn't have any feelings, good or otherwise, for Jake, but instead I found myself indifferent to his request. I knew, however, that I had better do as I was told. I glanced over at Arturo and he was watching us; if he had any thoughts on what Jake was asking me to do I could not tell from his expression. I slipped off the bed and onto my knees in front of Jake. I found myself looking directly at his crotch as he finished undoing his buckle and proceeded to unbutton his pants and pull down his zipper. As ashamed as I was that I had found myself getting caught up in this crazy situation, I had to acknowledge that I was not disgusted that Jake had asked me to suck his cock. With Arturo watching I hoped that he did not see the outline of my cock in my underwear as it started to get slightly harder.

"Now pull it out baby and get to work. Show me you haven't forgotten how to take care of Daddy," Jake instructed as he placed both of his hands on the back of my head, ready to force his soon to be exposed cock down my throat. He was wearing boxers and I reached in and quite easily found his already stiffening cock. I pulled his cock through the opening in his shorts and once again found myself looking at a grotesquely huge and thick black cock that was soon going to be in my mouth. Looking up into his face I could see a look of pure lust come across him. The smile was gone, replaced by a sneer of meanness that was looking to use the blond, white face that was now in front of him.

I reached out my hand, grabbing the base, flicked out my tongue and began to slowly lap first at the sides and then the head of the black monster. His cock was now swiftly getting harder and the thickness of it surprised me. It was obviously the same cock that had roughly used me the week before, but now it seemed almost larger as I continued to lick the sides and head. Once his cock was thoroughly coated with spit I opened my mouth as wide as possible in order to fit the now solid hard cock into my mouth. The spit helped, because even though I had my mouth open as far as possible, the sides of his cock still stretched my lips as I opened wide to take as many inches as I could. I didn't get very far, maybe only 2-3 inches, before the head of his cock would go no further. I then began to withdraw, so that once again I could try to impale the black tool deeper into my mouth.

"There we go boy," he said, as he started to apply pressure on the back of my head with one hand, trying to fit even more of his cock into my mouth. I had originally gotten on my knees and my back was pressing against the bed. When Jake started to push my head further onto his cock he also was pushing himself closer against my body until finally I found myself pressed against the back of the bed and my head was leaning back against the top of the mattress.

Jake wasted no time in taking advantage of the new position, taking his hand and pressing it on my forehead to keep it pressed firmly on the mattress. My arms were in front of me when I had started to suck his cock, and now in this position they were pinned to my chest as Jake's thick legs were now straddling my shoulders.

With each thrust of Jake's hips, I tried to relax my throat so I could take in more of his cock, but it was the thickness, not the length that was prohibiting me from taking any more of his cock down my throat. I tried to let my spit coat his cock even more but it did not do any good; pretty soon the spit was running down my chin and neck. Jake, however, didn't seem to mind that I could only take about half of his cock into my throat. He seemed content to be getting what I was giving, so I just relaxed and began to let him fuck my throat as hard as he wanted.

As he pumped my throat he found what must have been a good rhythm because he finally stopped staring down at his cock and began to look around the room. I couldn't tell from my pinned position on the bed what he was seeing, but something appeared to agitate him.

"Art, get the fuck over here and let me check out your ass. You can stuff all that shit up your nose later, now get the fuck over here and join the party."

"Jake, I ain't ready for this shit yet," I heard Arturo reply.

"I'm not going to ask you again. Now get the fuck over here and get on the bed." Out of the corner of my eye I saw Arturo come and sit next to me on the bed. I could see his expression was pure anger, bordering on rage. "And get the fuck out of those clothes. I want your ass up on the bed so I can taste that sweet ass of yours."

I caught a glimpse of Arturo as he slowly slipped out of his clothes. He stood there naked for a few seconds before finally crawling onto the bed. I could feel the mattress move as he climbed upon it and came to where my head was pinned against the mattress. I had the sense that he knew what Jake liked as he then proceeded to get on his hands and knees with his knees now straddled on either side of my head. I was now looking straight up at Arturo's cock and ass that were now only mere inches from my face. Jake's cock had not stopped fucking my mouth during this time and I was doing my best to keep my mouth open to take it in, while at the same time trying to breathe through my nose which was becoming increasingly more difficult.

Although Arturo's legs were somewhat hairy, the remainder of his body, at least from what I could see in my position, was fairly smooth. Because he was straddling my head, I could see all the way up the crack of his ass and except for a few small black hairs that surrounded his tightly closed hole, he was completely hairless. His stomach also was hairless except for a small trail of hair that ran down to his pubes, which I noticed had been trimmed. I could not tell if they had been shaved, or whether it was natural, but his balls were completely hairless as well.

And then there was his cock. It was beautiful.

It wasn't hard, but it wasn't completely soft either. I imagined watching me suck Jake's cock did a little something for him because his cock hung there, a good 7 inches at least, with the uncut head of his cock peeking out from beneath his silky smooth brown skin. Although Jake's and Martin's cocks were huge, they were also ugly, with thick veins and wrinkled skin. Arturo's cock though was smooth, and although there were also veins running through it they were not grotesque, but seemed to amplify its beauty. The color of his cock was just a little bit darker than his skin; I wondered immediately what it would feel like to have his cock in my mouth or in my ass.

"Oh yeah, that's what I wanted to see," said Jake, as he reached up with both his hands and pulled Arturo's cheeks apart. "That is the most beautiful hole I believe I have ever seen. God must have made this with his own hands, I do believe." Jake suddenly pulled his cock out of my mouth, then leaned his head forward and in one movement brought his face to Arturo's ass. He licked his ass from the bottom of his crack all the way to the top. He then did it several times more, starting at the bottom of his crack, right under Arturo's balls, all the way up through his crack and out at the top. He finally settled his mouth right over Arturo's hole and began to lick it with a passion.

My attention so far has been on Jake; I forgot about what Arturo was doing. I arched my head back a little further, no longer burdened with Jake's cock in my mouth, so I could see between Arturo's legs and up to his face. Arturo had his eyes closed and his head hung limply towards the bed as he held up his upper body firmly with his arms pushed against the bed. I wasn't an expert on such things, but I knew that Arturo was enjoying what Jake was doing to him. Arturo's mouth was slightly open and I could tell he was taking deep breaths as his chest expanded. I noticed his cock was getting harder, although not completely. Yes indeed, he was enjoying this a lot. I noticed that he was even starting to push his body backwards a little bit so that Jake could have more access to his ass. I began to wonder if Arturo's little straight act might be just that – an act.

Jake continued to suck on Arturo's hole for about a minute before slowly pulling back his head and then standing up. His cock was still hanging out of his pants and he carefully pushed it back into his boxer shorts and zipped up.

"Just a taste. That's all I need... for now," Jake said as he looked down at the both of us. He reached up with his forearm and wiped his mouth with his shirt. "And you," he said, looking at me. "...you get that fucking underwear off." Then without saying anything else he turned around, opened the door, and walked out closing the door behind him.

Neither Arturo nor I had moved and I found myself again staring at his ass and cock. Arturo hadn't moved and I could still hear him breathing deeply. I had the urge to reach up with my tongue and taste his cock, which was only inches from my mouth, but instead I carefully leaned forward as to make sure I did not touch him, then rolled over onto my knees and stood up. Arturo still had not moved, and as I looked over on the bed I saw just how beautiful his body was as he remained on his hands and knees. I had worked out and showered with many guys in school, and I don't think I had ever seen anyone that had such a perfect body.

I noted that his eyes were still closed and I wondered if he even realized that Jake had left the room. I also noticed that he was still pushing his ass back against the air, if only slightly. He clearly was still in his own little world, no doubt helped by what he had put up his nose.

"Hey," I said softly. Arturo still hadn't moved and after a few more seconds I raised my voice and repeated, "Hey!"

As if waking up from a dream Arturo suddenly jolted, rolled over, and then sat up on the side of the bed. He was blinking his eyes quickly as if he was having a hard time seeing. He started to look around the room again as if he suddenly had forgotten where he was. He again started to run his fingers across his shaved head.

He then noticed me standing there and after a few seconds he seemed to get some of his senses back.

"Fuck," he said, talking to himself. He then looked at me directly in the eyes and I saw an expression of anger cross his face. "If you ever tell anyone about this, I will fucking kill you." He then looked away, got up and went to where he had left his shoes and clothes on the floor. He then picked them up, folded them as best he could, and placed them next to the table on the floor. I noticed that my things were lying nearby and I picked them up and did the same, putting them next to his. I also took off my underwear as Jake has asked, leaving me now just as naked as Arturo.

Any hint of anger had appeared to dissipate as Arturo grabbed what was left of his cigarette, re-lit it with the lighter he had left on the table, and then went back and sat down on the bed. As he smoked with one hand he continued to rub his head with the other, leaning forward and looking at the floor.

Although we were both naked it did not feel all that strange; I had just sucked Jake's cock and Arturo had just had his ass eaten while I watched. We now didn't have anything to hide, as it was clear that we both had a role to play in this ongoing scene playing out by the minute. He may have thought of me as a 'fag' but it was clear he was going to have to do many of the same things I no doubt would be put through. What was still unclear was whether he had any capacity to secretly enjoy it, as I knew I was capable of.

I went and sat down next to Arturo on the bed. He still was looking at the floor and didn't seem to notice or care that I was sitting next to him. I had an urge to touch him, not sexually, but to just put my hand on him. I wasn't sure why I wanted to do this, but for some reason I could tell that I was not the only one in the room who felt the need to be comforted in some way, even if the gesture was a small one.

"So, what happens next?" I asked.

Arturo sat up slowly, looking at me again for the first time since warning me that I could never tell or face dire consequences.

"Man, I don't know," he replied as he looked around the room slowly. "The only thing I do know is that I am going to keep getting fucked up."

"What is that anyway," I asked, looking over at the table where there were still several lines of the powdered substance waiting to be inhaled.

"It's good shit," he said, suddenly laughing lightly. "Man, seriously you should try it. There's plenty more where that came from." I didn't say anything as Arturo slowly relaxed back onto the bed and began staring at the ceiling.

I got up off the bed and went to the door. Still naked I opened the door a few inches, making sure to stand behind it, and peeked out. I could see down the hallway to part of the bar area. More people had arrived. Most were black, but I noticed several white guys and a few guys who appeared to be Latino. They were dressed in regular street clothes, with the exception of a few black guys who were better dressed. One larger black man was wearing a suit. A few were just wearing wife beaters. It was definitely a mix of men from different backgrounds.

Most had paired off with one of the many women who were standing around. I could tell that these women were prostitutes, but not as dirty or sleazy as some of those that I had seen walking some of the seedy streets of Chicago. They were however in small, tight dresses, and the high-heels on many of them were several inches high. They all had long hair, including the black women, and even from my distance I could see their faces were plastered with makeup.

Some of the guys were touching the women in a not so subtle way. One taller black man wearing a black leather vest over a white t-shirt stood inches from a shorter blond woman with her back pushed against the bar. He was talking inches from her face with a sly grin. I noticed his hand was up and under her short dress and grabbing her crotch. She did not seem to mind. I did not see Martin or Jake and after 30 seconds I slowly closed the door.

As I turned around and once again looked at the room with the mirrors I wondered if anyone knew this oddly designed apartment was even in the building. I had been in the apartment next door and it was nothing fancy, and if anything somewhat dumpy. Yet here was this apartment, also in the basement of the same building, with no windows and decorated clearly for people who wanted to do nothing but drink, party, and have sex with no interruptions. I had not been able to see into the other two bedrooms as the doors were closed.

I wondered if they were also decorated in such a gaudy manner. Whoever owned the building no doubt knew that this strange apartment existed. I briefly wondered if Martin or Jake owned the building, or possibly if it was owned by one of their guests.

Arturo was once again heading toward the table and as I watched he inhaled another line. After doing so he seemed a little out of it for a few seconds. He then walked over to where I stood. He looked at me as he reached toward me, then behind me, and the next thing I knew the single light bulb in the room began to dim. I looked behind me and the light was on a dimmer switch. It had been on full, and Arturo turned it slowly to the left until there was still light in the room, but it was much less harsh.

"I'm going to lay down for a bit," he said as he walked back over to the bed, climbed up, and lay on his stomach. I watched him the entire way and I couldn't help but notice how fit he was. He had almost zero body fat, similar to myself, but he had more muscle tone. It may have been the light caramel color of his skin, but I could clearly see the muscles of his back and ass as he relaxed down onto the bed. He even had a slight tan line, as his ass was lighter than the rest of his body. I noticed my cock begin to tingle as I watched him bring his arms up to his shoulders to rest his head.

"You might as well take a break," he said, not looking at me. "Come and lay down with me."

I did as he asked and I slowly crawled onto the bed next to him, being careful not to get too close. The bed was king size and I was able to lie down and have some room to maneuver. I was on my side facing him with one arm pulled up where I rested my head. I watched as he lay there and after a few minutes I wondered if he had fallen asleep.

He opened his eyes suddenly, and looking over to me asked, "Do me a favor. Rub my back."

It sounded innocent enough and as I reached over I could hear in the other room that they had turned up the volume on the music that had been playing. I looked toward the door. I couldn't make out the song, but I could feel the slight vibration from the base as it rippled throughout the apartment. I also heard what sounded like a door closing and I wondered if one of the men had decided to take one of the women into the bedrooms.

I looked back at Arturo and his nude body lying next to me. I touched my fingers on his back and as I did his body shuddered. He let out a sigh and whispered, "Fuck that feels good." I began to rub my hands along the muscles of his back and as I did so he continued a low moan. I wasn't doing anything other than lightly rubbing his back, yet he clearly was enjoying the feeling of my touch. I made sure to keep to his back although my eyes were staring at the cheeks of his ass, which by this point I had determined were perfect in every way.

With the lights now lower I found myself starting to relax. I didn't for a moment forget that only feet away, in the other room, were complete strangers drinking and enjoying themselves. Laying there I found myself starting to wonder if this wasn't going to be as bad as I had first thought. My hand pressed harder into Arturo's body and I lightly started to squeeze and massage his shoulders. He continued to moan and I noticed that he was beginning to slightly grind his body against the bed.

"You know, you really should have some," he whispered without opening his eyes. I assumed he was referring to the drugs on the table.

"No, that's okay. I'm fine."

"It just feels good, is all I'm saying," he said as he continued to slowly move his body against the sheet. "I wouldn't let you fucking touch me unless I was high." He continued to let out the occasional moan. "Jesus Christ, I'm fucked up," he said and then suddenly rolled over onto his back. I could tell he was still quite out of it as he almost rolled off the edge of the bed, but caught himself and slid back toward the middle, getting even closer to me, where now our bodies were actually touching in several places.

When he settled back down I couldn't help but look down at his cock that was now clearly in view. It was rock hard. When Jake was licking his ass earlier I thought I saw his cock begin to get hard, but there was no doubt that what I had seen earlier was nothing compared to what I was seeing now. He was clearly rock hard to the point where his cock was not even resting on his stomach, instead floating about an inch above. The head of his cock was almost completely exposed from his uncut foreskin. It was the most beautiful cock I had ever seen. Comparing it to my own it may have only been an inch or so longer, but it was much thicker.

What made it truly beautiful was its silky smooth texture. It was the color of chocolate milk, and was just as smooth. My eyes were drawn to it and only after several seconds did I catch myself staring and quickly looked to his face to see if he had noticed. To my relief his eyes were still closed.

"Rub my chest," he whispered, eyes still closed, knowing that I would comply. I did as he asked and soon I was feeling his chest which was completely hairless except for a few thin black hairs that surrounded his larger than average nipples. My fingers lightly touched him at first, but then I let the weight of my hand fall completely on his body and I began to rub his chest, making sure that my fingers ran over his nipples. As I did, I noticed his cock begin to jerk upwards; the blood was definitely being pumped into his cock and my hands were making it jump on its own.

"So, you like what they did to you?" he suddenly asked quietly, keeping his eyes closed. "You faggots like this shit, don't you?" He asked it in a way that was not nearly as mean as it sounded. I got the impression that he didn't even think he was being rude by calling me a 'faggot' but instead was just curious and this was the only way he knew how to talk about the subject.

I thought about what he had asked and I wasn't sure how to answer. "I never did anything all that crazy until last week." I assumed he knew what had happened the week before but I wasn't sure. "I've been with other guys though, like friends from school. I guess I like guys, so yeah."

"That's cool."

"But last week when I met Martin and Jake", I hesitated before I continued. "...they were really rough but I let them do it." I wanted to explain to Arturo how I had somehow turned into this person that I didn't even recognize. I wanted to tell him, hoping he would understand, that although I liked what they did I didn't understand why I liked it. I didn't think he would understand, so I simply asked, "What about you?"

The expression on his face became sterner, as if he was thinking about something unpleasant. "I like to get fucked up. When I get fucked up I do shit, but it doesn't mean I'm a faggot. If they get me fucked up they know I will get stupid." He hesitated for a few seconds before continuing. "It doesn't give them the right to fuck with me though." He once again had a look on his face that was clearly driven by angered thoughts.

"Then why do you do it?" I asked.

He suddenly laughed, and it startled me. I stopped rubbing his chest for a second before he said, "Man, I don't know. It's just fucked up!" I could tell he was starting to get agitated. He quickly rolled over onto his side, facing me, and was now looking at me directly only inches from my face.

"You've got my back though, right?" he said suddenly.

I had been around a few guys who, when high, started to act a little weird. This was one of those moments. I didn't even know what he was talking about, but I told him, "Yeah, I got your back."

"Because it's just you and me. You understand that, right?"

"Yeah..." I said hesitantly.

"I watch your back, you watch mine. We got a deal?"

He was now so close that our foreheads were touching. I could see that his eyes were dilated. He was fucked up big time. "I got your back. It's a deal. You and me." I was winging it as best I could and I hoped he was not picking up on the fact that although he was probably one of the sexiest guys I had ever been close to I was still a little scared of him. I was scared of him when I first met him, but with him fucked up it added another dimension.

His face suddenly changed and his eyebrows pulled together in a worried expression. His mind had clearly shifted to something completely different. He pulled back a few inches so our heads were no longer touching and continued to stare directly into my eyes. He then grabbed one of my shoulders and pleaded, "Please don't tell my mom," and then he looked as if he were on the verge of tears.

I was now clearly out of my league.

It was bad enough that I was being practically kidnapped, but now I was in a room with a young kid completely fucked up and out of his mind. I looked over at the door and thankfully no one had entered. I didn't know what Martin or Jake would do if they came in now. It occurred to me that they most likely had seen Arturo very fucked up on previous occasions and I wondered what they had done to him. As I watched him start to get his composure back it angered me thinking about what those two assholes had obviously done to him to get him this screwed up.

Arturo's mind was apparently switching gears very quickly now as he no longer had a worried or sad look on his face, but instead had again closed his eyes and rolled onto his back. I noticed that his cock had remained rock hard, apparently having a mind of its own.

He didn't ask me to rub his chest but instead acted as if I wasn't even there. He started to rub his body with his hands, first on his chest, and then very soon he was grabbing his cock. He wasn't jerking off, but rubbing his hand over the shaft of his cock. With his other hand he reached down and grabbed his balls and started to pull on them. He was now writhing on the sheets in apparent ecstasy, even to the point where he was occasionally pulling his knees up and toward his chest. I noticed that he was also reaching down and switching between grabbing and pulling on his balls and then moving his hand down further and rubbing his ass.

As I watched, I couldn't help but get aroused at the show he was giving me. Even though he was clearly fucked up I couldn't help but enjoy the sight of such a dark and muscled Latino stud rolling on the bed next to me stroking his cock and ass. I wanted so badly to reach out and add my own hands to his, but I did not. I couldn't forget the fact that he was already quite fucked up after snorting some unknown drugs, but I didn't have to take advantage of the situation. I may have let myself get used a week earlier in ways that I would never have thought possible, but that didn't mean I had to become one of them. Instead I simply reached over and began to slowly rub the top of his head with my hand, noting the coarse feeling of his shaved head as I did so. I didn't think I was going to be able to soothe him out of his high, but simply rubbing his head wasn't going to do any harm either. He didn't seem to mind as he continued to rub his hands over his beautiful body.

We stayed like that for several minutes until Arturo appeared to grow tired and the pace of his movements began to slow down. I again couldn't help but notice that at no time did his cock soften, but instead remained rock hard floating above his body.

He eventually slowed down altogether and stopped. He just lay there with his hands to his side, breathing deeply. After a few more minutes I was sure he had fallen asleep and I was beginning to think that I might want to take a nap myself when he slowly opened his eyes and looked over to me. He had a content and relaxed look on his face. I couldn't tell what he was thinking but for the first time I saw someone who didn't look angry or worried. Gone was the tough guy mask that he had been wearing since we first met.

He began to slowly push himself up with one hand and with the other he reached over and lightly grabbed the back of my neck and started pulling it towards him. I didn't try to pull back and within seconds I was just a few inches from his face when he arched up with his head and closed the remaining distance between the both of us, pressing his mouth against mine in the process.

Part of me was shocked, but at the same time I felt this sense of peace as I felt his tongue slowly guide into my mouth. He wasn't being aggressive, but instead was very slow and sure with his movements. He continued to pull me down toward him until eventually my upper body was lying on his. He then reached up with his other hand and now had both hands on the side of my head as he continued to kiss me in a way that was more romantic than any other kiss that I had received in my lifetime. It was tender; it wasn't rushed; as he kissed me he moaned ever so lightly that I felt the vibrations coming from his throat.

His hands slowly moved down from my head to my back which he slowly caressed as he continued to kiss. At first I had kept my eyes open, but I now let them slowly close and allowed myself to fall easily and willingly into his embrace. I touched his tongue back with my own and I lightly sucked on his lips as he did the same with mine. Although I had one hand that was pressed between us I was able to use my other hand and I carefully and slowly moved it down his side. I soon felt his hand grab mine and he slowly guided it to his cock, which I did not hesitate to grab.

It was as hard as it had previously looked, and as smooth as cream. I did not grab it tightly, but instead I lightly guided my fingers around its base and moved my hand slowly up and down. With my fingers I found the head of his cock and gently pulled what remained of his foreskin down and then proceeded to rub my index finger over the tip of his cock. It was wet and I quickly was able to coat the entire head of his cock with his pre-cum.

He in turn had reached down and grabbed my cock. Because I was on top of him he did not have much range of motion, but as he grabbed my cock I couldn't help but let my own moan escape from my mouth. He grabbed my cock and held it in his hand giving it the occasional squeeze, all the while continuing to kiss me more deeply than I thought possible. I was in heaven.

Suddenly the sound of a door slamming behind me quickly snapped me out of our dream embrace. Arturo had also heard the door slam as he quickly began to push me away as I pulled away at the same time. As I rolled over, Arturo was already sitting up on the bed. I wasn't as quick but as soon as I began to sit up I saw Martin standing in front of the now closed door.

He must have come in quietly when we were kissing as neither Arturo nor I had heard him. I wondered how long he had been watching before he had slammed the door to catch our attention.

"Well, well, what do we have here?" he asked with a smile on his face that did not hide his obvious glee at catching us in the act. Neither of us said anything, and instead we both scooted to the edge of the bed to stand up.

"Just stay where you are," Martin commanded. We stopped, our legs hanging off the bed and resting on the floor. "You," he said, looking directly at Arturo. "Maldito is here and he wants to see you. Get ready." Martin then turned around, opened the door, walked out and closed it behind him.

Quickly coming out of my daze I looked toward Arturo to see if he knew what was going on.

"Who is Maldito?" I asked.

Arturo did not say anything, but simply stared at the now closed door. The look on his face was clear. He was terrified.

~oOo~

It had been only a few minutes since Martin had left the room. I had remained in place, sitting on the edge of the bed, not knowing what to do. Martin had indicated that some guy named Maldito had arrived and wanted to see Arturo. I had no idea who this 'Maldito' was but clearly Arturo did and it had him concerned.

He had gotten up from the bed and started to pace the room slowly, his head down, looking at the floor with a worried expression locked in place. A few minutes earlier he had appeared to be somewhat out of it due to whatever it was he was snorting up his nose. He was now much more focused, although I could see in his half-closed eyes that he was still feeling the effects of the drugs. As if coming out of a dream, Arturo suddenly looked up and saw himself in one of the many mirrors, shook his head, realizing that he was still naked, and walked to where he has tossed his jeans and started to put them on. He had just put his second foot through his jean leg and was pulling them up to his waist when the door opened.

Into the room walked the biggest man I have ever seen in my life.

As he walked in I couldn't help notice that the top of his head cleared the doorframe by mere inches. I also noticed that he was not only tall, but wide as well; his shoulders appeared to come close to brushing the sides of the doorway. He was dressed in a dark blue, pinstripe, two-piece suit, with a red floral pattern tie. I had been to my father's office many times and I knew an expensive suit when I saw one; this man was dressed to kill. His shoes were black and shined to the point where the single light bulb in the room glared off their tips. He was wearing dark sunglasses and as he walked in the room he slowly pulled them off with his right hand, folded them, pulled his jacket open, and slid them into the inside suit pocket. He was wearing black leather gloves that he removed and put in his other suit pocket.

The Man knew how to make an entrance.

He only walked a few feet into the room when he stopped and said, "Check the room."

I then saw movement and behind him came two smaller men who proceeded to enter the room. By smaller it was only in comparison to The Man who had just entered before them. They were each easily over 6'2" and as thick as tree trunks. They were dressed in suits, sunglasses, and black leather gloves as well. The three of them made quite the threesome.

One man went to the left, and the other to the right, as they slowly walked around the room. One checked the desk as the other leaned down on one knee and looked under the bed. As the man leaned down his jacket opened slightly and I could clearly see a gun that was holstered on his belt. I had been around hunting guns growing up, but I had never seen a gun like this. All I could see was that it looked powerful and had something screwed on the end. I wondered if it was some type of silencer like I saw at the movies. I looked at the other man and I assumed he had a similar gun as well.

I watched silently as one of the men went to where I had put my clothes and proceeded to look through the pockets. The other went over to where Arturo had finished putting on his jeans and proceeded to pat him down the same way a cop would pat down a criminal. I evidently posed no threat as they ignored me completely. Still, I found my hands moving over my crotch in a meager attempt to pretend as if I was not sitting on the bed completely naked. I would normally have felt horribly embarrassed sitting naked in a room with three fully dressed men, but the whole day had been so bizarre to begin with that I was beyond the embarrassment stage and was now entering pure bewilderment.

When they were done searching the room they walked back to where The Man was still standing. With his glasses now off I could see that he was Latino, had a trimmed and neat goatee, and looked to be in his early 40's; I couldn't be certain as his skin was smooth and had very few wrinkles.

Without saying anything they both nodded their heads in unison at The Man, in what I sensed was some type of silent 'all clear' message.

Without looking at either man, The Man simply said, "Leave." The two men again walked around their boss - one to the right, the other to the left – and exited the room. With what little I witnessed of the two as they searched the room, I did not doubt that they were very well trained bodyguards, although to what extent I did not know.

The second man to leave began to close the door and hesitated for a second as The Man gave a final instruction:

"Watch the door, do not let anyone in, and do not interrupt me."

With that the door closed and it was now just the three of us alone in the room.

I looked over at Arturo who was slowly connecting the remaining buttons on the front of his jeans. He was looking down as if he did not want to acknowledge The Man who was now towering in the room over us.

Looking at Arturo the man said, "Hola, Arturo."

"Hola," Arturo replied, still looking down.

"Hola?" The Man asked, with puzzlement in his voice. "Is that all you have to say to me? Just hola?"

The Man then walked slowly to where Arturo stood. With his right hand he reached out and lightly grabbed Arturo's lowered chin and raised it so that he could look directly into his eyes.

"Arturo, I have told you many times how I want you to address me. Have you forgotten already or are you just being disrespectful?"

"No."

"No, what?"

"No, Tio."

A smile slowly stretched across his face as he reached out and grabbed Arturo's shoulders with his huge hands, holding Arturo out as if he was being inspected. "Ah, that is much better. Your father would be very upset if he knew his son did not show respect to family." He then pulled Arturo's half-bare body into his own and proceeded to squeeze him tightly into the biggest bear hug I have ever seen.

I watched silently as the two men embraced, or more accurately The Man was embracing Arturo as Arturo's arms had remained at his side. I saw that the top of Arturo's head was no higher than The Man's chest. Earlier I had the chance to see Arturo from head to toe and he clearly could hold his own with any normal sized man. Arturo's body was ripped with natural muscle and he was not short by any means. I was no shrimp myself, but looking at the two together amplified just how huge The Man was. Although Arturo's arms remained at his side I knew that he would not be able to reach completely around The Man if he had tried to hug him back.

After several seconds The Man released Arturo momentarily, only to turn him around and pull him against him once again, his right arm now draped around Arturo's bare chest.

The Man bent his head downward and continued his conversation with Arturo.

"It has been a long time since I have seen you, Chico. I have missed you so much but you do not look very happy to see me. Do you think your uncle would not notice such things?" Looking around the room again and settling his eyes on the desk where the mirror still lay he continued. "Maybe it is that stuff that you put up your nose. You know I do not approve of such things. They are for cabrones and not for family."

I could see the beginning signs of anger cross his face: lips tightened, eyes becoming focused on nothing, but intense nonetheless, when suddenly he closed his eyes, took a deep breath, and slowly leaned his head forward... and kissed Arturo's head lightly.

In a tender and gentle voice that sounded foreign coming from such a man, he said "It saddens me that you are not happy to see me. Have you not missed me at all?"

Although I was only a few feet away from where they stood I could barely hear Arturo as he whispered, "I have missed you, Tio Maldito."

So this was Maldito, and he was Arturo's uncle? I didn't want to show the surprise on my face, so I sat there and said nothing. I did wonder why his uncle had called him Arturo *and* Chico; I assumed it was some type of nickname.

As I continued to absorb the reality of what I just heard, Maldito remained still, not moving his head, still pressed against Arturo's. His eyes were closed and the expression on his face was as close to real sadness as any that I had seen. Here was a towering man who spoke with a commanding presence with his henchmen. Yet here he was, holding Arturo in such an intimate manner that I felt even more uncomfortable sitting naked in their presence, if that was at all possible.

"Have you forgotten all that I have done for you, Chico, since your father left us? Although I am not your true Uncle, I have always been there for you and even if we are not related by blood, I am the closest thing to a real family that you will ever have.

"You and your mother had no one, but I was there for the both of you after your father died. I took care of you when you were just a boy and I loved you like you were my own." As he said these words his arm that held Arturo's chest began to caress it lightly. "And please do not call me Maldito. You know that name is only for those with whom I do business. It is a name I am not proud of, but need for those who must understand that they dare not cross me. For you Chico, I am simply... Tio."

So he's not his real uncle? I puzzled.

"Si, Tio," Arturo replied, his Spanish coming out in pieces. "I will never forget what you have done for mother and myself. I just wish you did not see me like this. I am not proud of what I have done. I thought I was smart, but I was stupid. I wanted to be like you, but I made mistakes and I feared you would no longer have anything to do with me."

"Oh, Chico, I will always be here for you. You are family to me and nothing comes between family. You should know that by now." Maldito looked up, around the room and the surroundings. "However, I must confess I do not approve of what your new friends have asked of you. I will speak to them tonight, but they have told me what you have done. I cannot demand that they stop this, as it was not of my making."

As Maldito spoke I could see a look of shame fall across Arturo's face. His eyes still appeared dimmed by the drugs and it looked as if he was close to tears, but he managed to hold them back. "I wish you had come to me earlier and told me of your plans as I would have told you to not get involved and to go back home to your mother. But you are no longer a boy. You have become a man and your mistakes are your own. One day maybe you will look back on this and it will make you stronger. Only time will tell."

"I really have missed you, Tio. I wanted to see you so bad, but I was too ashamed." Arturo reached up and with both of his hands he grabbed Maldito's arm that was wrapped tightly across his chest. "I love you, Tio." With that the tears did start to flow and his body became limp, but remained tightly held in place by the strong and huge arms now holding him up.

"Compose yourself, Chico. Everything will be fine eventually. Plus, you are here with me now and I have wanted to see you for such a long time. I want to enjoy this time together, so no more tears."

Arturo was taking deep breaths, and appeared relieved for the first time since Maldito entered the room. Maldito once again was standing up tall, still holding Arturo against him, and was once again looking around the room.

To my horror his eyes came to focus directly on my own.

"And who are you, may I ask?" he said in a tone that although was calm, was at the same time terrifying.

"Adam," I said.

His eyes closed slightly, as if thinking he did not believe me.

"No, that is not your name," he replied, still staring at me intently. "I will ask you again. What is your name?"

Confused, and not understanding, I opened my mouth to speak but nothing came out.

"I will tell you what your name is, as you appear to be confused. Do you understand?"

"Yes," I replied, still not understanding.

"Your name is No One. I repeat. Your name is No One. Let me hear you say your name now so that I know you understand."

"My name is… No One," I replied, hesitantly.

"And where are you now?" he asked.

Again I hesitated to answer, not understanding.

"You are nowhere. Do you understand? Your name is No One and you are nowhere. For the rest of your life if anyone asks about anything that you see today you will say nothing because you are No One and you are nowhere and because of that you know nothing. If, after I leave today, I hear the name Adam, I will know that you have forgotten the name I have given you, and if you have forgotten your new name you may have also forgotten where you were today, and if that is the case then I promise you I will find you and you will wish that you had not forgotten what I have told you. Do you understand?"

"Yes, I understand." And I did understand.

"Arturo, is No One a friend of yours?" asked Maldito.

"Yes, Tio, he is a friend. I will make sure he remembers what you have told him."

Again, Maldito looked at me. "Now that we understand each other, I want you to get up and go sit in the corner on the floor. I do not want to hear a word from you. You will sit there and remember your name and remember where you are and I will forget that you are here. And I expect you to do the same. Now, go sit."

I didn't hesitate and quickly stood up and went to the corner of the room closest to the door and sat down, crossing my legs and resting my back against the wall. Because the bed was in the middle of the room with mirrors on all the walls, I could see Maldito and Arturo multiple times from almost every angle.

Oddly, I felt as if I wasn't even in the room, but instead was watching what was happening as if I was having a strange out-of-body experience. I'm not sure if it was the way that Maldito made it clear that I could never discuss what was happening, or whether I was just still in shock as to what I had just witnessed. But I found myself watching the two of them as if I were nothing more than a camera lens focused on the two men standing before me.

Maldito had once again focused his attention on Arturo and as I watched he bent down and still holding his arm across Arturo's chest he bent down and kissed Arturo's neck lightly, pulling back just a few inches and whispering into his ear, "Do you remember many years ago, when I would come and spend the days with you and your mother. We would go to the beach and I taught you how to swim? Do you remember those days?"

"Yes, Tio. I remember," Arturo replied, still running his hands up and down his uncle's arm. "I was so proud that you would want to spend time with mother and me."

"I could never replace your father, Arturo, but I do try very hard to love you as much as I know he loved you. You look so much like him. It hurts me sometimes to look at you as it does remind me of the pain of losing a man I always considered my brother. But then I am happy that you are still here, with me, and I hope you love me as you would have loved your father if he were still with us."

"I do love you, Tio. I was so afraid you would not want anything to do with me." Arturo gently pulled himself away from his 'uncle' and turned to face him. "I remember the casita and how safe you made me feel..." Arturo's voice trailed off, thinking of things that I could only imagine.

"Do you want to go back to that time, years ago, Chico?"

"Yes, I want to Tio. I just want to know you truly forgive me for what I have done."

"I had already forgiven you Chico. Know that. I was hoping we could spend some special time today and it would not be just business with your new acquaintances. No one will come in the door. I promise you Chico that we will be left alone. You will be safe with me."

As I sat silently I was mesmerized by what I was hearing. Just a few hours earlier I had met this Latino kid wearing baggy jeans and a wife beater shirt, who had a tough exterior to match. Watching him now though I no longer saw the tough, hard edged young man, but a kid who appeared almost childlike in the presence of this huge man.

I watched as Arturo walked behind Maldito, again noticing how huge the man was, and as Arturo came behind he reached up, his hands barely able to reach, and began to pull the jacket off Maldito's immense shoulders. The jacket slid down his arms, and with it now in his arms Arturo carefully folded it in half and walked over and laid the jacket on the desk. He then walked back to the bed, and now standing in front of Maldito, he reached up and gently started to disassemble the man's tie until the knot came undone and Arturo was able to pull it off completely. Again he walked over to the desk where he carefully folded the tie and set it down on the desk.

"You do remember, even though it has been many years, Chico," said Maldito. "But back then I had to get down on my knees so you could reach my neck. You were so much smaller back then. But now look at you. You are a man and I no longer need to bend down for you. I am so glad that I came here today Arturo, to see the man you have grown into."

Arturo reached up to unbutton Maldito's collar. "I dreamed about you, Tio, for many nights. I thought I would never get to see you again."

He continued to pull apart the buttons of the dress shirt and as he did so I was able to see the first glimpses of Maldito's neck, which appeared to be the same light caramel color as that of Arturo's. Arturo began to pull the end of the dress shirt out of the other man's waist so he could undo the remaining buttons. When he finished with the last button Arturo reached first to Maldito's right wrist, and then to the left, removing the cufflinks. I could not be certain but the cufflinks looked to be real onyx and silver. Although a huge man, he was apparently someone who was just as big on style.

Arturo then reached up and with both hands he slowly pulled the shirt off Maldito's body. Although I tried to remain as motionless as possible I could not help that my eyes widened at what I saw.

With his shirt now off, Arturo walked over, folded it carefully, and set it on the desk. I barely noticed Arturo walk to the desk as I was hypnotized by what I saw. As I expected his muscles were huge but not in the grotesque way that I often saw on bodybuilders. Instead, Maldito's body was thick with muscle, but it was not ripped and cut with veins pushing out from the skin. Instead the muscles were solid, smooth, and did not give the impression of someone who went to the gym out of vanity, but instead of someone who epitomized pure strength and true masculinity. His biceps were the size of my legs and his stomach, although not a six-pack by any means was still flat and solid and no doubt I could walk across them and he would most likely not even notice.

But what caught my attention even more than his massive and hypnotizing physique was that his chest, arms, stomach and back were completely covered in tattoos. With the exception of his hands, neck, and head, there was not an inch of his upper body that did not have a tattoo carved into his skin. When he had been dressed you could not see any tattoos, but now that he no longer had a shirt it was like the suited and huge businessman had been replaced with this muscled and tattooed gangster god. If it had been an earlier era, he no doubt would have left an impression that, over time, would have turned his existence into one that would feed the myths of lesser men, that there was a time when Gods did in fact walk the earth.

I could barely make out the details of the tattoos but of what I could see were multiple crosses, naked women, dragons, and what I thought at first was the US flag, but noticed there was only one star. I quickly thought to where I had seen such a flag before. It was on a trip I had taken years earlier to San Juan and I remembered that it was the flag of Puerto Rico. There were no doubt gang signs also, but I would not have known what they were. I had seen men before who were covered in tattoos but none of them came close to pulling off what Manito achieved;

which was giving an impression that no one would ever forget. Combined with his huge size, and his tattooed torso, anyone who met Maldito would no doubt never forget the time and place they met such an incredible beast of a man.

With his shirt now removed Arturo began to lightly rub his hands over Maldito's chest, appearing to trace some of the tattoos with his fingers. I watched as his right hand settled on a very detailed picture of a man's face that was drawn on the large man's chest. Arturo brushed his fingers over the man's face and a look of sadness came across his face.

"As I told you Arturo, your father will be with me always, as will you one day."

Arturo leaned forward, and having to push off slightly with his toes to get the necessary height, he brought his lips to the smooth chest and kissed the tattooed image of the man.

He then pulled back, brought his feet back to the ground, and then slowly he bent at the knees until he was kneeling. He reached up again, this time to the larger silver buckle, and began to pull at the leather.

Maldito reached down and gently grabbed Arturo's hand. "Chico, if you continue you must understand that you are no longer a boy, but a man and I will treat you as such. I will not make you do anything you do not want... if you stop now. I will take care of this business and leave, and trust me when I say that I will not be mad at you. But know that if you do continue, I will expect you to obey me and do what I say, from this point forward. I cannot guarantee that I will be able to stop myself once we begin."

With his smaller hand still held by Maldito's massive paw, Arturo looked up and said, "I have dreamed about this for a long time, Tio. I want your love so much that I will do anything for you. I have worried for so long that I would never see you again; worried that you had forgotten me. But here you are. I cannot risk losing you again. I want you to stay. I will not disappoint you." He then bent forward and rested his forehead on the fabric of Maldito's slacks. Pulling back and looking upwards again he said, "I will not break, Tio. I will be strong for you and I will make you proud of me, I promise." He then brought his head forward again and pressed his cheek against the massive legs.

Maldito looked down at his Arturo and said nothing for several seconds. "I hope you do make me proud, Chico. Now show me what your new friends have taught you since we have last seen each other."

"Sit down so that I can take off your shoes and undress you fully."

Maldito walked to where I had just been sitting and sat on the bed. His weight crushed the mattress and it let out a loud squeak of submission. Arturo stood, and then standing before his adopted uncle he began to once again remove his jeans. He quickly unbuttoned them and let them slide down to his ankles and stepped out of them. He was now standing fully nude, and hard once again, but this time in front of Maldito who was now half undressed himself. He then slowly turned around, showing his naked body from all angles, until he faced the large man once again.

"They have taught you much, I see."

"Yes, Tio."

He stood only a few seconds before getting on his knees and began to untie his adoptive uncle's shoes, pulling them off one-by-one and then doing the same with his socks. He then reached up and again started to undo the belt. With the belt undone, Arturo unclasped the hinge of the slacks, grabbed the zipper, and pulled it down. With his slacks now undone Arturo reached down and pulled on the pant legs. Maldito helped by pressing his hands to his sides and lifting his weight off the bed allowing the slacks to be pulled off completely. Once again Arturo carefully folded the slacks and getting up walked over set them on the desk.

Not surprisingly I thought, Maldito was wearing boxers that ran halfway down his thighs and I briefly wondered where a man would buy boxers this huge as my own would no doubt not even fit on one of his legs. As Arturo returned to the bed, Maldito stood up and Arturo once again went down to his knees. When he stood up I thought I had seen some movement in his boxers, but surprisingly I did not see anything poking up from the cloth.

Even sitting up on his knees, Arturo had to reach his arms above his head to get his fingers around the edges of the large boxers, and with his head at the level of Maldito's thighs he began to pull them down.

From my angle in the corner I could see directly in between the two as Arturo's hands pulled the boxers down to the point where I first saw Maldito's jet black pubes. He continued pulling downward and I saw the first glimpse of the base of his cock. Even from my distance I could see that the thickness of Maldito's cock was thicker than my own wrist. As Arturo continued to pull down the boxers, and more of his adoptive uncle's cock was exposed, the thickness of his cock did not diminish, and if anything it looked to be thicker in the middle.

Arturo had the boxers down far enough where I could now clearly see his entire huge bubble ass, but still his cock had not yet come completely free. Finally, with the boxers now almost halfway down his thighs, the head of Maldito's cock finally came into view. Arturo then quickly pulled the boxers down to the floor where Maldito quickly stepped out of them.

I was already transfixed at the length and thickness of Maldito's cock before I even saw the head. As expected he was uncut, but instead of his cockhead thinning at the end, it instead exploded in size. When I toyed around with some of the websites men used to hook up, I often found guys who would describe their cock as having a 'mushroom' head. When they posted pictures what I found more often than not was that men used this description to make up for the size of their cock in other areas. I saw pictures of small cocks where the head was bigger, but by no means would anyone describe the cock as 'big' or 'huge'. This was not the case today. What I saw hanging from Maldito's waist was not only the biggest cock I had ever seen, it was the biggest head on a cock I had ever seen. I doubted he would ever think of describing his cock as having a mushroom head, or if he did describe the size he would describe it in the way that I thought more fitting, which was that it was the size of a fist.

As I sat there in a trance-like state I watched as Arturo reached up, and with both his hands he grabbed Maldito's cock. Even with both his hands clasped on the massive thing hanging between those tree trunk thighs, I noticed that still more than half of the cock was exposed. It was only then when I realized that his cock was still not hard.

"I'm ready for more, Tio. I want more. I've thought about it for so long and there has been no one like you, no one even close."

"I believe you, Chico. I know more about what you have been doing than you know. I have always kept an eye on what you were doing. As I told you earlier, I do not like what you have been doing lately, but maybe in some way it has prepared you for today. I am looking at you now and I see a young man that has filled out nicely. You will of course never be as big as your Tio, but very few men are."

As Maldito finished talking Arturo's hands kept rubbing the huge cock that was hanging in front of him. He reached forward with his mouth and brought the head of the massive cock to his mouth. There was no chance that the cock would fit in his mouth, or anyone else's for that matter; it was simply too big. But still Arturo kissed it and eventually brought out his tongue and licked at the sides. The foreskin was still wrapped around the head of his cock, and as I watched Arturo opened his mouth wide and sucked in a mouthful of the dark brown skin. I had seen porn where a man would suck a guy's balls into his mouth and this looked very similar, but instead of balls filling and bulging inside Arturo's cheeks, it was just the foreskin of Maldito's massive cock.

Arturo continued to suck and munch on the hefty skin that was wrapped around Maldito's still hidden cockhead. After just about a minute Maldito reached down, grabbed Arturo under his arms, and as if he didn't weigh an ounce, pulled Arturo off his knees and set him back onto his feet.

"Although that feels good, Chico, and I do love to look down at you as you do it, I do not enjoy my cock sucked. I learned years before I hit puberty that I was both blessed and cursed and that I would never feel the warmth of a mouth taking all of me in. So instead come lay with me on the bed, will you?"

Maldito then walked to the side of the bed, laying down on his side, and moved to the center of the bed. His feet hung off the edge of the bed by more than a couple of feet. "Come sit on my stomach."

Arturo climbed on the bed and lifting one leg he stretched his knees and thighs wide as he straddled the man. As he climbed on top I continued to watch from the corner, still able to see everything that was now taking place on the bed

~oOo~

Arturo was straddling the huge body so that his face was directly above Maldito, staring into his eyes. Once again I found myself in awe as I saw the size difference between the two. In order to have his head level the big man, Arturo was so far up on his body that I could clearly see Maldito's belly button directly behind Arturo's ass. I also noticed that although Arturo's legs were stretched wide his knees did not touch the mattress, and in essence his entire weight was resting on the giant's upper torso. As I watched, Arturo put his hands flat on the mattress on both sides of Maldito's head in what appeared to be an attempt to take some of his weight off. I doubted Maldito noticed the weight on top of him any more than a full-grown man would feel the weight of a cat as it napped on his chest.

I looked down and saw that Maldito's cock was still soft and had fallen sideways against his right thigh. I wondered if Maldito suffered from what I head other men suffered who also had big dicks, which was that they often had a difficult time getting hard. When Arturo had been sucking on his foreskin it did not appear to respond to the attention either. Now, as Arturo straddled him, I saw that his cock was still huge, but still quite soft.

As I watched, Arturo leaned his head forward and carefully pressed his lips against the smooth large lips below him. He did it with some hesitation, as if he was concerned Maldito would turn away. He had no reason to be concerned as Maldito reached up and with his right hand he grabbed Arturo's head from behind and pulled it down to his own. As I watched his lips wrapped around Arturo's and smothered them with his own. The way Maldito kissed him was not as tender as I expected, but Arturo did not seem to mind and began to kiss with even more enthusiasm.

With his other hand Maldito reached up and began to stroke his back, rubbing his hand up and down Arturo's lean and fit muscles. After only kissing for a few seconds I could see Maldito's body start to move slowly and begin to gyrate. He removed his hand from the back of Arturo's head and now with both hands he began caressing Arturo's back with more gusto. At first his hands were mostly at Arturo's shoulders, but slowly Maldito's hands moved lower and lower until he had grasped both of Arturo's ass cheeks and began to pull them apart.

It was then that I noticed that his cock was no longer resting limp on his thigh.

As I watched Maldito's cock, I couldn't help but think of the many times my family had gone to my grandparents' farm. They owned a huge house in the country and it included a barn where they raised a few horses that the family would ride for pleasure. They had a few mares and a gelding but they also kept one stallion for breeding. I remember walking through the stables one day when they were putting the mares back in the barn after an afternoon ride. As they walked the horses I happened to notice the stallion and I saw the horse 'drop'. What had just been a soft mound of tissue was suddenly this two-foot long massive thing that was jutting and bouncing in all directions. It was so startling at the time but apparently it was very normal to everyone else and I did not ask what was happening. As I now sat in the corner, watching as Arturo ran his tongue over and into the large man's mouth, and Maldito was pulling Arutro's ass cheeks apart with his massive figners, I saw Maldito's cock do almost the exact same thing that I had seen the stallion do years earlier.

Without touching it, his cock first rolled off his thigh and then very soon it began to lengthen and stretch; within 30 seconds it was rock hard and pushing up against Arturo's asshole, which was now very exposed due to the large hands pulling his cheeks apart. His cock looked like it was starting to bend, pushing against Arturo's hole, and as if he had done it hundreds of times before, Maldito reached down with his right hand and quickly lifted his cock so it was no longer poking at Arturo's ass but instead rested on his lower back.

I had measured my own cock and I knew that I had 7 solid inches when hard. What I saw resting on Arturo's lower back was more than double what I had in length and even more so in thickness. I had heard that there were men out there that did not do porn, that kept to themselves, that did not brag about their size, but had cocks that were 15 plus inches. I never believed they existed; I thought it was purely the fantasy of men who dreamed of such men. A week earlier I thought that I had ran into two freakishly huge black men. However, looking at the smaller frame of Arturo straddling the huge man, I knew that the true freak of nature was on that bed, and I wondered if Arturo had any idea what he was getting himself into.

Maldito's body had continued to grind underneath Arturo and his hands had begun to grab Arturo's ass cheeks harder and harder. It had started subtly between the two of them but within a few minutes I could tell that the testosterone was flowing heavily between the two. Not only was Maldito's body starting to grind harder on the bed, but Arturo had started to gyrate his hips and push them back against the monster cock that he surely could feel rubbing against his back. Eventually Arturo reached back with one hand and grasped the cock around the head.

"Oh my god Tio, you are so big," said Arturo, who clearly was surprised as he pulled his head back and sat up.

"You told me you would not break, and I believed you. I will not be able to stop myself much longer if we continue. Are you sure you want what your Tio is offering as much as you say? I can promise you that you will never forget this day if we continue, and that your life will change in ways you cannot imagine."

I watched Arturo's face as he hesitated a few seconds. I wondered if the thoughts that were going through his mind were the same thoughts I had just a week earlier. He was definitely getting to the point of no return and I could see his mind racing with both lust and fear. We had not had the chance to talk about it but I had no doubt that he had also been Martin and Jake's boy toy, along with who knew how many other guys he had been forced to have sex with. His earlier 'straight' act was clearly in doubt, but the odd relationship between him and Maldito appeared to be more than physical, or at least it was not purely sexual. I clearly did not understand the complex relationship that they had when Arturo was younger, when he had apparently lost his father and Maldito had stepped into his and his mother's life. But as I watched Arturo earlier, when Maldito first entered the room, I saw someone who wanted more than anything to have forgiveness and approval.

What I saw happening on the bed now though was clearly becoming much more complicated, as both men thought through the consequences of their actions if they proceeded forward. I watched as Arturo struggled with conflicted feelings, and after a few seconds that seemed like minutes, Arturo apparently had come to his decision.

"Make me a man, Tio. Make me *your* man."

With that he again leaned forward, and no longer holding back his feelings, both mental and physical, he proceeded to kiss with a passion that bordered on frenzy. I briefly wondered if he still felt the effects of the drugs he had been snorting earlier. I doubted if they would have left his system so soon.

Maldito also picked up the pace, kissing Arturo in return just as aggressively.

"So you want to be my little man, Chico? So be it. I will show you how to be a real man."

Suddenly Maldito lifted his right hand and brought it down on Arturo's ass. His hand was so big that it easily covered one of Arturo's ass cheeks completely, and where it landed I saw a red mark begin to surface almost immediately. I could see the jolt of surprise pulse through Arturo body as Maldito's hand landed.

"You have awoken me, Chico. You will not be able to calm me now." I saw his hand pull back again and he brought it down hard. "You may have thought you had been taught obedience by these thugs, but you do not know true obedience. You will learn this today." Again, he brought his hand down on Arturo's ass and once again I saw Arturo's body go tense. "A boy becomes a man only when he has been tested by a better man. Only then will you know what it is like to be a man in a man's world." Again the hand came down and the sound of the smack made my body wince. "You may rule others, but only after you have been ruled yourself. Your obedience will instill the same in others, but you will only learn by giving in to me first. Do you understand, Chico?" Again, the hand came down hard on Arturo's ass, which was now as red as blood.

I watched Arturo as a look of determination came across his face. He was listening and with each smack his eyes would briefly open wide in pain, but they would not close. He continued to look directly into Maldito's eyes, never turning his gaze away, as the giant man explained his version of how the world worked and how men like him worked within it.

"I will break you, Chico, even though you may think you cannot be broken. It is because I love you that I will do this. I will not hold back and you will thank me for it" He paused for a few seconds before continuing. "If not today... one day."

Maldito brought both his hands forward, and pressing against Arturo's chest he pushed the boy upward so that he was sitting upright. Maldito stopped grinding his body and reaching to his side he grabbed both of Arturo's wrists in his own and pulled them tight in front of him.

"As I look at you now I can't help but see your father in your eyes. You look so much like him that it pains me to know what I must do."

He then brought his hands together and using just one hand he easily held both of Arturo's wrists together.

"I will do to you what I did to him many years ago, when he was no older than you. He hated me for it... for a time. I was only 8 years older than him, but he had no idea what was waiting for him once he got away from the home that I alone had made for him. He thought his father provided for him, but he provided nothing. It was always me that provided for him and his family... and you."

I saw that Arturo was listening, but the look in his face began to show signs of concern, and also confusion.

"Your grandmother took me in after my father was murdered. I was only 10 and your father was a mere baby, but I had already seen a cruel world that took no mercy on anyone, including my own father. Your grandmother raised me as of her own. You see, she had known my father when they were younger. They were lovers, and if she could not have my father, then she could at least have me in his place.

"Her own husband, your grandfather, was a fool and a coward. He had no idea how the real world worked and I soon realized that although I had lost the only family I had, I still had to look out for my *new* family, as they would surely perish if not for me.

"Your father had no idea that the roof over his head and the food on his plate came from me. From me doing terrible things to people who paid me to do such things. He didn't see the things that I had to do, instead believing the lies that his mother repeated and the silence of his father who let such lies go unchallenged. His father, your grandfather, was weak. I saw in your father a man who would also be weak unless I showed him a world where it was not pretty, not simple and definitely... not easy."

I watched as Arturo just listened, saying nothing, while his so-called uncle rolled to the side, keeping Arturo's hands in one of his own. Arturo soon was on his side as well, having slid off the huge man. He was on his side momentarily before the man who he had treated as his uncle simultaneously pulled his hands above his head and used his free hand to roll Arturo onto his stomach. Maldito had managed to keep Arturo in the center and head of the bed, and the way that he did it was seamless, as if he had done it many times before.

"Your father would not talk to me for several years. Did he ever tell you that? No? I'm not surprised. As much as I had hoped he would listen and learn from me, and to understand the blood that ran through *my* veins. I should not have been surprised when he did not. You see we did not share the same proud heritage of *my* father. A man he did not know, but someone from whom he would have learned so much. Oh, Chico, there are so many things you do not know."

Maldito reached up and grabbed Arturo's wrists once again. He first pulled them to his side, and then behind his back, where once again with one hand he held them together in a grip that I doubted even the strongest man could release himself from.

"I tried again and again to get your father to see the world the way it really is. He may not have been my brother by blood, but I raised him as if he was my real brother nonetheless. He was family, the only family I still had to call my own. But he refused to listen. Instead he continued to play a small man's game and one day he was sloppy; he did not do his homework, he did not understand that he was running with a crowd that would spot his bullshit so easily. That was the day your father did not come home and it will be a day I will never forget. I failed him, and because of that I will never forgive myself. "

Arturo's head was to the side and I could barely make out his words.

"I didn't know. Why are you doing this?"

Keeping his hand firmly wrapped around Arturo's wrists, Maldito now picked up his knee, lifting it across the bed. Their positions now reversed, as he now straddled his adopted nephew.

I had been listening to their conversation so intently that I did not notice Maldito's cock. I looked down from his face and I saw that it was now rock hard; the length went from beneath Arturo's balls to several inches above the top of Arturo's upturned ass cheeks, resting heavily on his lower back.

"I told you that I was keeping watch over you. I always have ever since your father died. You don't know how disappointed I was when I found out the petty crimes you were involved in. But I kept my distance, hoping that you would learn that your choices were ending in nothing but bad consequences. I hoped you would eventually change your ways. But you did not learn. Instead you continued to make poor decisions until one day I find out your judgment was not as good as I had hoped. Even worse I find out you are being forced to do depraved things… with these Negritos no less. Do you know how just walking into this shithole has made me sick to my stomach? Do you know how careful I had to be to arrange just to come here and find out for myself if you had indeed fallen as low as I had heard?"

"I'm sorry, Tio. I thought you said you had forgiven me." The look on Arturo's face continued to show confusion, but in addition betrayal had been added to the mix, as he realized this man he had pretended was his uncle was not quite as forgiving as he had first let on.

"Oh, Arturo, I have forgiven you. I have not lied to you with anything that I have said today. But I fear forgiving you may not be enough. I had a chance years ago to save your father and I did not. I will not make that same mistake today. You will learn to obey, and then, and only then, will you stand a chance at rising to the level of what I expect from you. And if to get you to obey I must have you fear me, then so be it. If I did nothing, you would be found in a ditch one day, with a bullet in your head... or worse. I will not let that happen again... not to family."

Suddenly Maldito looked to where I still sat motionless.

"You, No One. Go to the door and tell one of my men that to bring my bag." I hesitated for merely a second. "Now, No One. If I have to ask you again you will not be pleased."

I quickly got up and walked to the door that was only a few feet from where I sat. I opened the door just a crack and standing in the small hallway were the two goons who had previously been in the room. They were both standing in a position that sent a message to anyone at the party that this room was to be avoided at all costs.

"He wants his bag," I said in a low voice, hoping that no one else would hear me but the two men. The man closest do the door turned his head slightly in my direction, nodded, and then reached behind him and closed the door. I stood there for a second before turning around and walking back to my corner.

"I think he's getting it, sir," I told Maldito, with my head down and making sure that I did not make eye contact.

"Thank you, No One."

I began to sit down when Maldito spoke once again.

"Please, come sit on the chair, No One. I was harsh with you earlier but it was not you who I was angry with and I apologize. So come, sit."

I did as he told, and walked to the other side of the room where the desk was located and sat on the chair that was next to it.

"I may also need your assistance, so please do pay attention, No One."

In my new position I was much closer to the bed, only a few feet, and I could see Arturo up close as his head was turned to his side facing me. His expression had not changed. He was still very aware that the man he had thought was his uncle had turned the tables on him and that he was in more trouble than he first imagined. Our eyes met briefly, but he looked away quickly. I thought that once again I saw a look of shame come across his face as he waited for Maldito to proceed with his plans.

I heard a noise and looked over to see one of the men walk in the room and in his hand was a black leather bag. It was small, no longer than two feet in length, with a zipper that ran across the top and between the two handles.

"Put it next to me, on the bed," Maldito requested, and the man did as he was told, and then quickly turned around and walked out of the room. At no time did he appear shocked or surprised at seeing his boss naked and straddling the young man.

"No One, open the bag please. Better yet, bring the chair over here so you are closer."

I stood up, bringing the chair with me, and sat next to the bed as he requested. I reached across to the bag and pulled the zipper open.

"Be careful, No One. When I ask that you get me something be sure to get only what I request. You could hurt yourself if you are not careful and accidently grab something that you should not. Now, look in the bag and give me my handcuffs. They are not metal like the ones you see on TV, but are soft and black and made of Velcro."

I pulled the bag apart so that I could see inside and I easily spotted what he wanted, but I also saw things that I wish I hadn't. There were silver and sharp things that one would expect to see only in their worst nightmares. Just like his two accomplices he also had a gun in the bag, similar to the one I had previously seen. As I reached down to grab the handcuffs I made sure to not come close to the scary instruments... or the gun. As I pulled out the handcuffs I saw that they were made of nothing but fabric and the two holes where the wrists went were sewn together in the middle. I handed them to Maldito, who took them and quickly pulled the Velcro back from each wrist restraint. He placed Arturo's wrists in the holes and then pulled the Velcro straps tight, so that when he was done Arturo's hands were now tied tightly behind his back.

I sat back in the chair and as soon as Arturo's hands were bound. Maldito rolled to his side, facing Arturo and myself. He kept his right hand and arm across Arturo's back and started to gently run his hand up and down his back, including his ass.

"No One, there is a container with a lid. Please get it, take off the lid, and set it next to me."

I looked in the bag and there was a black canister the size of a small coffee can. I pulled it out and screwed off the lid. Inside was what looked like a clear jelly but I couldn't tell what it was. It did not have any smell. I set the canister next to Arturo where I knew Maldito could reach it.

Talking again to Arturo, Maldito continued.

"Are you ready to be my man, Chico? It does not matter, because I will take you even if you are not. Very few men can take me without screaming. Do I need to worry that you will scream, Chico?"

"I don't know, Tio. You are scaring me."

"You should have thought about that earlier. Too many men get in over their heads, and every time they do not realize it until it is too late. Maybe now you will think twice before getting into situations where your only hope is that your Tio will come and save you. Do you want to be saved, Chico?"

"Yes, Tio, but I can take care of myself. I promise."

"You say this, but I'm looking at a boy who I have tied up and is on his stomach and is unable to move. I do not think you can take care of yourself at all, Chico. But what is it that people always say? Ah, yes. It is never too late to learn new things. Today we will see if that is indeed true."

Maldito reached over and with two of his large fingers he reached into the canister and scooped up a gob of the clear liquid. It was thicker than it looked, and he was able to get a couple of tablespoons of the goo on his fingers. He then brought his hand over to his adopted nephew's upturned ass.

"Now Arturo, it is time for you prove to me if you are indeed a man, or the boy I have been hearing about who needs his Tio to come and save him. If you want me to stop, simply tell me. However, if you are indeed a man who can now take care of himself, I want you to prove it."

He then put his two fingers against Arturo's hole and started to spread the lube around it.

Still looking at Arturo's hole and not looking up he said, "No One, is there still some of that stuff my nephew likes to put up his nose?"

"Yes, there is still some on the mirror," I said, looking over and seeing the two lines that Arturo had prepared earlier.

"Bring me the mirror, then."

I got up from the chair, picked up the mirror, making sure that I did not spill the powder, went back and sat down, and held the mirror out to Maldito.

Maldito reached over with one of his greased up fingers and ran it down one of the lines. Up close I realized just how big his hands were. They were over twice the size of my own and just one of his fingers was as big as some of the cocks that I saw swinging from between men's legs at the gym. The powder easily stuck to his finger. Without any warning he then took his drug-coated, cock-sized finger and quickly jammed it up Arturo's hole.

"Aye, Tio!" yelled Arturo, as his body immediately went tense.

"I thought you liked this, nephew? I hear you can't go a day without your little powdery friend? What would your father say if he could see you now?" Maldito quickly pulled out his finger and I could see that most of the powder was no longer there. He then reached over and once again ran his finger down the remaining line of powder, and bringing it back to Arturo's ass he plunged his huge finger back into the hole that was now not only coated with lube, but with a powder mix that appeared to be dissolving into the liquid, and into Arturo's ass.

"Please uncle, it stings!" Arturo begged.

"And do not think I am stupid, Chico. I know that you do not just put this stuff up your nose. I hear that you have learned of quite a few tricks where you can put this stuff. I understand that you do many crazy things when someone else supplies you with what you want. Is this not true?"

"No, Tio. I never do anything but snort it. I only take it when I want, Tio. I always pay for my own. I never let anyone do anything that I don't want." Arturo's breathing had become more rapid and he continued to have a stunned look on his face.

Maldito bowed his head for a moment. "Arturo, do you think I would accuse you if I was not certain?" He continued to keep his finger in his 'nephew's' hole and began to push it in and out as he continued to speak. "Did you know that those Negritos have proof of what you have done? Do you know how I ashamed I was when they showed me?" He continued to fuck his adopted nephew's hole with his finger and suddenly he jammed his other finger in.

Arturo turned his face into the bed and moaned loudly. I was not sure if it was in pain... or pleasure.

"They even thought they could get me to pay them and threatened that they would show this to people who I do business with. I listened to what they had to say and even smiled in agreement that, 'of course I could not let anyone see my nephew in such compromising positions.' It would be shame to my family... and of course bad business.

"I agreed to give them the money they requested, which was a small amount, but they were too stupid to know that the money they requested is nothing to me. They are small thugs and do not know who they are dealing with. Like your father, *they* have not done their homework. If they had, they would never have approached you, let alone came to me afterwards. You do business with fools, Arturo."

Maldito began to not only push and pull his fingers, but also twist them side-to-side in Arturo's hole. Arturo kept his face down and continued to groan. I did notice that his ass cheeks were no longer clenched, as they first were when his uncle plunged his lubed finger in his hole.

"So I come here today, not only to close the loop into this mess you have created, but also to try one last time to show you that there is only one person who can save you now."

He reached over again to the jar of lube and this time he scooped up an entire handful. He brought his hand to his cock and ran the palm of his hand down his huge manhood, covering the top of his massive cock from the base to the head. He then began to twist his hand around his cock, coating the lube on all sides. He needed to reach over again into the jar to get more lube to finish the process until his entire cock was now glistening with lube.

"Are you ready, my little adopted nephew? You say you have dreamed of me, but this is no longer a dream. I wonder if in your dreams you found yourself screaming?"

Arturo slowly turned his head to the side. I could see his eyes had once again begun to gloss over. There was even a small amount of drool that was dripping out of his mouth and landing on the white sheet.

"Uncle, I promised you I would do anything for you. I no longer care if I live or die. But if I must die, I pray that it will be at your hands, and no other's. Just please forgive me, Tio. If I know that I have your forgiveness I will never betray you again. And if I must give my body to you to find forgiveness, then I beg that you take me now. Please, Tio, fuck me and forgive me."

As he said these things I saw that his ass has begun to move underneath his ex-uncle. I had wondered if the drugs would have some effect as they were put directly into his ass. As I watched him begin to grind, pushing his ass back toward the large piece of meat resting on his hole, I began to realize that they most likely did. Again, I looked into his eyes and although they were open I could tell they were focused on nothing but whatever feelings he was generating in his mind and his hole.

"You say you want me inside you. We will now find out."

Maldito started to lower himself in position, and realizing that Arturo was too high on the bed he reached down, and with both hands he lifted Arturo's hips completely off the bed and moved him a good foot lower on the bed. The back of Arturo's head was now underneath Maldito's massive chest, but his ass was now lined up with the monster cock that was now rock hard and coated with lube.

Lowering himself to his elbows and grasping the top of the bed with his hands he looked over to me and demanded, "No One, guide me into my nephew, will you?"

Maldito's knees were resting on the bed and his hips were poised in the air. Even with his hips pushed off the bed, his cock still hung down and was touching the bed right below Arturo's now greased and drugged up hole.

I reached forward with my left hand and grabbed his cock several inches behind the head. I could not get my fingers around it, not even close. I had thought the two cocks that ravaged my hole a week earlier were huge, and they were, but this was nothing like them. If combined, the two black cocks would be close to the thickness of this Latino monster I held in my hand.

I lifted his cock off the bed and I could feel the actual weight of it. Maldito moved slightly as well to help position himself as I brought the head of his cock and positioned it at the entrance to Arturo's hole. As the head pushed through Arturo's bubble cheeks my eyes widened when the reality of just how big Maldito's cock was compared to the smooth, small bubble butt beneath it. The only thing that I had seen come close to what I now saw before me was when I watched videos of some guys getting fisted. You would see the fist and you couldn't imagine it going into the hole, but eventually it would. I rarely watched those types of videos because I thought they were just too freaky and there must be something incredibly wrong with guys who got into such things. Now, however, I was going to see something even worse.

"Here I come for you my little one," Maldito said. Looking over to me again he continued. "And No One, do not let go of me. You will need to hold it tightly in place otherwise it will slip and it will not go in. If you need to you can use both hands. Just do not let go."

I did as I was told and I clamped down harder on Maldito's cock, but if it hurt him he did not show it.

I could feel the pressure as Maldito began to lower his weight, and his cock, onto his 'nephew.' As he had predicted I had to use the muscles in my arm to keep the cock from sliding away from Arturo's hole. It was harder than I thought. As he continued to lower his body I could see his cock pushing against Arturo's ass, and the mattress begin to press down underneath Arturo's waist.

I looked at Arturo's face and he started to come out of his daze as he felt the massive cock press down onto him. His eyes widened and I could see the muscles in his arms start to engage as he tried to move them. I wondered if he had momentarily forgotten that his hands were handcuffed behind him as he continued to try and pull his hands apart. I noticed that his ass cheeks were once again clenching closed, trying to keep his uncle's cock from going any further. He tried to scoot up on the bed using his legs but Maldito quickly brought his own legs together, in essence pinching Arturo's legs together with his own and removing any chance he had to get away.

"Ahhh...Tio! It's too big Tio! It's too big!" Arturo began to yell.

"I do this because I love you Chico, not because I enjoy it, although you do bring back so many memories of your father. He tried to get away from me like you are now. You have done many men Chico, but you have not taken a true man until now. As I said earlier... you will thank me for this one day."

I felt the pressure of Maldito's cock push harder... downward and it took a surprising amount of strength for me to hold his cock in place as it wanted to slide away from Arturo's hole which continued to fight back.

"I told you that I would stop if you asked, but I don't think I can stop now Chico. I want you too much."

My arm was shaking to hold his cock in place and I was ready to reach in with my other to stabilize it, when sudden there was a slight give and I felt Maldito's cock move forward several inches.

Even with his adoptive uncle's body locking him into place I saw Arturo's body tighten up like a board. Out of his mouth escaped not a scream but a moan, so guttural that I doubted I would hear such a sound again for the remainder of my life.

I looked to where Maldito's cock met his adopted nephew's ass and the head of his cock had slipped in entirely. Arturo's ass was now spread apart with a cock that was several inches buried in his hole. Again I thought back to those few fisting videos I had seen but instead of an arm jutting out from his hole it was a horse cock that was wide enough to keep his ass cheeks spread entirely apart.

"Are you still with me, my dear Chico?" asked Maldito.

Arturo continued a low moan, his eyes open, but staring into nothingness. I'm not sure if he even heard Maldito.

"There are many who pass out with me in them, Chico. I am so proud that you are not one of them. Although it would not be necessary that you be awake, but even so I'm glad that you are. Now, let me see if you are still in one piece."

He then pulled back suddenly and with an audible *pop* he pulled his cock roughly out of his Arturo's ass. This time Arturo did scream, although it was short and ended with him closing his eyes for a few seconds where I thought he might have in fact passed out. However, after a few seconds his eyes opened again and he continued to moan. I noticed there were now tears streaming down his cheeks and face and his moaning slowly turned into a light weeping noise.

I watched as Maldito lifted himself up and off Arturo's body.

"No One, please look and tell me if you see any serious damage?"

I had to lean in close as the lube was still coating his cock and it was difficult to see if there was anything else mixing in with the lube. I also needed to get a better angle to I could see Arturo's hole.

"No blood," I replied, although I could see that Arturo's hole was purple around the edges, puffy, and looked raw.

"Ah, that is good. We can now continue then. Are you ready for more, Chico?"

Turning his head sideways as far as possible so that he could look at his 'uncle,' Arturo replied, "Tio, I'm sorry. Please, I'm so sorry." His words came out choked, as if his throat had also had been ravaged.

"If you are truly sorry you will take all of me in. You need to stop fighting me now, and always. Once you do that I can promise you that you will never fear anyone, or anything, again. You will know that you can do anything and you will never, ever, let yourself get used by anyone other than someone who truly loves you. Do you understand, Arturo?"

I was still grabbing Maldito's cock and noticed that it had remained as solid as marble. I wondered if some of the powder could have possibly been absorbed into Maldito's cock, and if so, what it would do.

"Do you promise you'll always love me, Tio?"

"I do promise, Chico. Now show me that you want me once again inside you. Maybe that powder that you so love is starting to work its wonders on your hole, no? I am not as ignorant to what boys like you do with this powder. I do not approve, but if it makes it easier to take your Tio, then I will allow it. "

He turned and then looked to me. "Rub his hole with my cock, No One. Let me see if he is truly ready for more."

I lifted his cock once again and positioned it on Arturo's hole. I started to rub his cock on Arturo's hole, moving it up and down and in circles.

"Now Arturo, if you promise to stay in place I will untie your hands. I know this is uncomfortable for you, but you must promise me that you will not try and get away."

"I promise, Tio," Arturo replied meekly, but what also sounded like some relief in his voice.

Maldito reached down and with his right hand he pulled the Velcro apart, which allowed Arturo's wrists to become free.

"Now grab the edge of the mattress in front of you and do not let go. Do you understand, Chico?"

"Yes, Tio."

Arturo then slowly moved his arms from around his back and then reached up and grabbed the top edge of the mattress with his hands. Once again I noticed the size difference between the two, as Arturo's arms were stretched out straight but Maldito was still on his elbows, both holding on to the edge of the mattress. I noticed that except for his legs, which were pinned between the larger man's legs, Arturo's body was completely covered by Maldito's shadow.

"Show me, Chico, that you want more. Let me see what these Negritos have taught you."

Even though his face was still streaked with tears, and he looked like he was on the edge of exhaustion, Arturo started to grind his hips and ass against the monster cock.

"That's good Arturo, but show your Tio that you really want it."

I saw Arturo's fingers grip the edge of the mattress harder and he started to move his hips with more rhythm and what appeared to be an actual lust for the cock that had nearly split him in two just a few minutes earlier.

"Your new friends, they say that you have fucked many men at once, and that you beg them for more. They say that you do not even care who fucks you. Is that true, Chico?"

There was a look of shame again as Arturo thought how he would answer.

"I have uncle, but I don't understand why I do it, and it's only been when I'm high. I feel bad later, after I realized what I've done. But I don't remember everything. It's very fuzzy when I do those things."

"But that hunger when you are begging for men to be inside you... do you remember that now? Do I bring back any of those feelings, Chico?"

Arturo had continued to move his hips, and I had kept the pressure of Maldito's cock on his hole.

"Yes, Tio. I remember how hungry my ass feels when so many men use me. It's starting to feel that way now. I just want more and more and I can't help myself. It is a hunger that never goes away."

"So, tell me then, Chico. What do you want me to do now? Be careful though, because I may just do it..."

Again, Arturo looked over his shoulder as far as possible so he could look at his adoptive uncle. Any earlier shame was clearly gone and in its place was a lust, a true hunger that I had not seen before other than in myself when I looked in the mirror a week earlier as I gave in to men who would do anything they wanted with me.

"Fuck me, Tio. I am ready to be a real man and I will prove to you that I can handle all of you, Tio."

Arturo's gyrations were now in full swing and I was amazed at the difference between just minutes earlier when he was begging his uncle to stop and here he was now begging for his uncle to continue.

"Fuck me, Tio. And I want it hard. Make me learn to take it, Tio."

I continued to hold Maldito's cock securely as once again I felt him shift and get in place.

"I think you are ready also, Chico. But it is not just you and I, Chico who are here. Let me ask your friend." Looking over at me, and this time I did not look down as our eyes met, he asked. "So tell me, No One. What do you think I should do?"

I looked at the entire view in front of me. The previously cocky Latino teen who had met me at the park earlier was now on his stomach, his legs squeezed together, his hands gripping the edge of the bed, and a look of crazed lust on his face mixed with his tears. I looked at the man who towered over him, covered in tattoos and muscle, his horse sized cock positioned at the edge of Arturo's hole that was now quivering and shaking. I looked back at Maldito, and with a serious but honest voice I told him what he should do.

"Fuck him. Fuck him hard."

And with that Maldito looked back down at Arturo who was still looking over his shoulder and said, "You heard the man."

He then pushed forward and I felt his cock slide through my fingers as I held it in place. Again Arturo's ass did not give in easily. The bed squeaked as the weight and force of Maldito's cock pushed through Arturo's body and into the mattress. I watched as Arturo's head turned to face the mattress and again he buried his face in it.

"More lube, No One," Maldito asked, and I quickly removed my hand and grabbed more of the clear goo from the container before bringing it back and coating the huge cock. I pushed my fingers to the head of his cock also where I did my best to coat its now uncovered head.

And that's when it started to disappear into Arturo's body.

The low moan escaping Arturo's mouth returned as the head sank into Arturo's hole and the puckered and purple edges once again stretched to an unbelievable length in all directions. I watched as the edges of Arturo's hole closed around Maldito's monster head as it slipped past. Arturo's breathing picked up dramatically as if he had just run a 40-yard dash in 10 seconds. He was still moaning and the sound was thick and raspy as if the sound was coming from somewhere deep within his body. His tongue hung out like a dog as he gasped for air.

Instead of pulling back this time, Maldito continued to lower his weight and his cock, onto and into his adopted nephew. Although Arturo's legs were pinned together, I saw them bend at the knee as inch after inch of Maldito's cock sank deeper into his ass. Arturo's body began to shake and I watched his knuckles tighten their grip on the mattress.

"Tio... Tio... Tio!" Arturo mumbled louder with each inch. His head and neck began to arch back as if he were being shot with a Taser. I saw him briefly let go of the mattress, his fingers stretched wide and shaking, before once again grabbing the edge of the bed.

"I love you Chico. Never forget that," Maldito said as he continued to gut Arturo with his cock.

Half of his cock was now in his nephew's hole. I noticed that I no longer needed to hold the monster cock to keep it in its place. I carefully pulled my hand away, but continued to lean forward, literally feeling the energy that was emanating from the two.

"I... love... you... too... Tio," said Arturo, his eyes now rolling in their sockets.

The massive cock appeared to be hitting some barrier inside Arturo's hole, and Maldito began to shift his hips slightly side-to-side as if he were trying to find a better angle for his cock to go deeper. He did this for a few seconds before smiling and exclaiming, "Ah, there you are," and as I watched his cock once again began to sink deeper.

As he lowered his body further, Arturo's hamstrings once again convulsed and his legs curled at the back of his knees to the point where his heels were pressing tightly into the back of his adoptive uncle's thighs. It looked like he was once again trying to pull away but it did no good. He was pinned even more than before as his Maldito's body was now pressed down even more on his smooth backside.

Arturo continued to breathe heavily, but this time he was exhaling quickly with his lips curled into a tight circle. I had seen this type of breathing before but it was when I watched a video of a woman giving birth and she was in the last stages of contractions.

"So close now Chico. So very close. You are doing very well. I am so proud of you."

Arturo arched his neck but looking straightforward he replied, "Thank you, Tio. I am trying so hard, Tio." Each word came out of his mouth as if he were struggling to say each word.

"Not much more. I promise. But Chico, before I am completely inside you I want you to do something that would make me feel so good. Would you do one thing for me? If you do this one thing I think I will fall in love with you like no other."

"Yes, anything," Arturo replied. I looked at Arturo's face and I wondered if he even knew what was going on. His head still jerking, and his eyes still rolling back in their sockets occasionally. He looked as if he was going slightly mad.

"When you were just a boy and you would nap by my side I would pretend you were my son. I have never told anyone that. It has been a secret I have always kept to myself and I thought I would die with that secret. Would you do me the courtesy of pretending that I was your father, if just for one day? Call me father and I promise I will never leave you again."

I saw Arturo's eyes suddenly close and his head stop arching backward. He turned his head toward me and I saw his face melt. Gone were the straining muscles and gritting teeth. In their place was a face filled with calm as if he had just woken from the most fabulous dream. With his head now resting on its side he opened his eyes and although I don't think he was looking at me purposely, his eyes were still locked onto mine.

His words came out in a whisper, but they were clear and loud enough for both of us to hear.

"Take me, father. That is all I've ever wanted."

Maldito pushed forward and the remaining 5 inches sank in. I sat back momentarily in total bewilderment that his cock had actually gone all the way in this little Latino ass that was right in front of me.

Arturo's body first went rigid again, then collapsed as if he had just been given a dose of shock treatment. Then slowly his body began to shake; not a lot but enough to look as if he were freezing cold and he just couldn't get warm.

And then Maldito started to fuck him.

After such a careful entrance - or as careful as one could be with such a freakishly huge monster cock – I had expected Maldito to start and fuck slowly, but he did not. He pulled half of his cock out in about two seconds and then just as fast he shoved it back in. Arturo's body once again stiffened, his punishing groans returned, and his tongue once again fell out of his mouth as if he couldn't control it.

Again Maldito pulled back halfway and plunged back in, this time just a little faster. Arturo looked to be on the brink of passing out, his eyes beginning to flutter.

Again and again Maldito pulled about halfway out and plunged back in, getting faster and faster with each stroke, until he was fucking Arturo at the pace of about two thrusts per second. Arturo's moans had turned into garbled grunts and occasional bursts of whining like a puppy. But he did not ask for the abuse to stop. Instead he appeared to be barely balancing what sanity he had left, with what was left of his rational mind. He would occasionally look directly ahead at the mirror in front of him, and as if noticing what was happening to him he would look directly into his own eyes and try to make some sense out of what it was he saw.

As Maldito continued to fuck Arturo he continued talking to him as well.

"Ah, Mijo, I so love you. You feel so good. Do you like your Papi inside you like this?"

"Si, Papi," Arturo grunted in reply.

As I watched Arturo getting fucked, I saw his eyes once again momentarily become focused. He was looking into the mirror and I now saw that he had locked eyes with Maldito, whose ass was lifting up and down and plunging his massive cock into his hole.

"I want more, Papi." Arturo said as he locked eyes with Maldito. As he did I saw him push upwards with his ass as the larger man pushed down, as if he did not have enough cock in him already. Maldito responded by pulling even farther back with his cock with each withdrawal and slamming to his balls as he came back down.

I saw a slight moment of hesitation as Arturo momentarily tried to pull away from his uncle, but he quickly regained himself and pressing lips together he one again pushed up and back against his adoptive uncle.

"You do love me, don't you Chico."

"Si, Papi, more than anything. I know you want more so please, Papi, give it to me."

Maldito did not need to be asked twice and in one move he pulled his cock all the way out of Arturo's ass. For just a brief second, as I heard Arturo yell once again, I looked and was able to see the hole that had once belonged to Arturo, but now clearly belonged to Maldito. The lips of his ass were still purple, but more so. Even from a few feet away I could see that as Maldito pulled his massive cock out, what looked to be part of Arturo's insides momentarily came out with the cock. His hole instinctively tried to close and I could still see the dark redness of Arturo's insides for just a second. Suddenly Maldito plunged his cock back into his adopted nephew's ass and did not stop until it was buried as far as it would go.

Arturo's head jutted back in an arch so angled that I thought for certain his neck would snap. He looked like he was screaming but no sound escaped his mouth. Without waiting Maldito once again begin to pull his cock quickly out of Arturo's ass until once again I saw the head pop out, the redness of Arturo's insides at the very edge of the hole, and again the cock slammed forward until there was no further for the cock to go.

Maldito's strength was amazing as I realized that with each pull backward and thrust forward he was lifting practically his entire body weight. I had wondered how much Maldito weighed when I first saw him enter the room, but now as I saw him up close, and I saw the muscles of his back and abdominals kicking in, I realized that he surely weighed over 350 pounds. As he came down he literally was crushing Arturo's body into the mattress.

When I first saw the redness of Arturo's insides I wondered if he was bleeding, but as I continued to watch Maldito pull all the way out and pushing all the way back in, I could see that miraculously he was not bleeding at all, and that the redness was most likely his guts showing through the gaping hole his uncle was making of his now very abused asshole. It still tried to close each time his uncle pulled out, but not by much, and I briefly thought that I could easily fit my entire fist in Arturo's hole. I kept those thoughts to myself though as not to give Maldito any ideas.

I saw the sweat was starting to break out over Maldito's body and that drops had begun to fall on Arturo below him. His breathing had started to pick up either from the excitement of the fucking, or from the enormous amount of energy it must be taking to fuck so rough. I gathered it was a little of both.

As I watched him fuck Arturo, I saw that Arturo was once again apparently transfixed on the image of himself in the mirror. I began to wonder, "What if that was me? Could I take that?" And as I watched as Arturo's body clearly had switched gears and was now pushing back against each of his uncle's thrusts, I saw that his brain was most likely exploding in ways that maybe, just maybe, I had gotten a taste of a week earlier. I started to pretend that it was I on the bed and that it was Arturo watching me getting fucked, and without even being aware of it I started to stroke my cock. Maldito, however, did notice.

"No One, are you enjoying this as well?" he asked, verbally shaking me out of my fantasy.

"Yeah…" I wanted to say more, but nothing came out.

"Maybe one day, No One, but today is for my new son. But when you are ready to cum you let me know and I will tell you what to do. Do you understand?" He said all of these things as sweat was running down his face and as he continued to fuck Arturo.

"I understand."

"Good," he relied.

For the next 5 minutes I watched an assault of a man that was not even close to any of the porn that I watched in the early morning hours when my parents were asleep. Not even the fisting videos compared. I was watching something so brutal, but at the same time so unbelievably unique, that I could not look away. If anyone walked in they may have turned away in horror to see someone being as brutal as I saw Maldito was being with Arturo. However, Arturo never once let go of the side of the bed or pulled away. I was seeing a man break another man in a way that only a man could... and I thought it was beautiful.

My mind and body were racing, and I was sweating, when all of a sudden I knew that I would start to cum within seconds. Not forgetting what I had been told, I called out to Maldito in a voice louder than I had expected. "I'm going to cum soon!"

Maldito suddenly pushed himself off his elbows and sat up on his knees, his cock flopping out of his nephew. He reached over to where I sat and with both hands he grabbed me under my shoulders and lifted me up as if I were a doll. He pulled me over to where he was sitting and pulled my back against his chest, and wrapped one of his arms around my chest so that I was now in front of him and on my knees as well. For a brief moment I panicked, thinking that he was going to push me over on my hands and knees and begin to fuck me; instead he moved back several feet on the bed, taking me with him. I was now looking down at Arturo from the same angle Maldito had been fucking him.

Not sure what was happening, Arturo had begun to get up on his elbows. Seeing what he was doing Maldito quickly told him, "Stay down, Miho. Get back down and do not move." Arturo did what he was told and was once again lying flat and grabbing the edges of the mattress.

In the shock and confusion of being pulled onto the bed, my need to cum subsided slightly, but my cock was still very close and on the edge.

"Fuck him, No One, and cum in his ass. Do it now." He said it in a tone that was not harsh, but very clear that I was not to hesitate. He let his arm drop from my chest, which caused me to fall forward and onto my hands. I found my cock was now only inches from Arturo's hole, which was truly now a hole that was as open as a Red Bull can.

I looked up at the mirror and saw that Arturo was looking at me. As I was looking at him he pushed his ass back and before I could react he has pushed his ass all the way back and my cock quickly was buried to my balls.

"Do what he says. Fuck me," Arturo said.

With another quick glance in each other's eyes in the mirror I didn't waste any time and I soon found myself starting to pound away at his hole, which was so loose, but at the same time so warm and moist. I had been close to cumming but I did my best to fuck his ass for a good minute. I knew that all I had to do was let down my guard and I would cum, but it just felt so damn good that I didn't want it to stop. I had never felt anything like it. It was so sloppy, but it made it just that more exciting to know that my cock was in an ass that had just been wrecked by one of the biggest cocks I knew I would ever see in my life.

I was so overwhelmed at how my cock felt that I didn't even realize that Maldito had picked up his cock and was now resting it on my ass and back, just as he had done to Arturo earlier. For just a split second I hoped he would take me, that he would throw me down and do what he did to Arturo.

As if he could read my mind I felt Maldito lean forward from behind me and whisper in my ear, "I must admit, No One, that there is something special about you that intrigues me, but I dare not, at least today. Maybe just a small gift so you do not forget me." I then felt him move back so I could continue to fuck his adopted nephew, but I felt like the most special person on the earth as I felt Maldito's huge hands start to caress my ass, and lightly press one of his greased up fingers against the edge of my asshole and slowly push it in.

That was all I needed.

I started to explode inside of Arturo's ass as he continued to push back against my cock as if he was trying to suck my cum out with his hole. I wasn't nearly as composed as I had hoped and I let out several yells of pleasure as the cum continued to shoot out of my cock and into Arturo's now ruined hole. My body continued to jerk a few times before my orgasm subsided and I found myself starting to collapse on top of Arturo. I felt Maldito's finger slip from my ass.

Before I could collapse completely, Maldito once again was grabbing my hips and carefully this time lifted my body and rolled me next to Arturo, where I collapsed on my side facing the two of them.

"That was good, No One. Now, you will stay still as I finish." He looked me in the eyes as he said those words, and although it was very quick I saw one of his eyes wink at me, as if we now we had a secret that was to be kept between just the two of us.

Maldito once again moved back up on the bed and got himself in the position where his cock was pointed and pressed against Arturo's ass.

"Are you ready, Miho for me to give you the best gift you will ever receive?"

"Si, Papi, I am ready. Can I get up on my hands and knees so I can push back against you?"

"It is harder to take that way, Miho, but if you want me to fuck you that way, I will oblige."

Maldito pushed himself back up until he was sitting on his knees. When he did Arturo slowly pushed back and I watched as he winced, feeling his muscles and bones once again given the chance to move freely.

When he pushed back onto his hands and knees I saw a smile cross Maldito's face. It took me a second to realize what made him so amused. I looked at Arturo, now waiting for his ass to be used once again.

I looked at Maldito and due to how big he was, his cock was a good foot above where Arturo's hole was now waiting. Even with Arturo pulling his knees fully together to give his ass as much height, he still was not high enough to reach his uncle's cock. Arturo did not seem to have noticed, as he appeared to be waiting for the next onslaught of unbelievable fucking.

"Look up, Miho. You see why I fuck the way I do? Although you are a grown man now you still have quite a ways to grow before you are as big as your Papi."

Arturo looked up and saw what his uncle was talking about and began to let himself go flat once again on the bed.

"No, no. Stop, Miho. I will give you what you want. I will show you another way, but stay where you are. I hope you have strong arms and shoulders, Miho."

Arturo pushed back up and as soon as he did Maldito reached down and this time grabbed Arturo's hips in both of his hands and pulled him off the bed and back against his stomach, but unlike me he lifted Arturo clean off the bed where his knees no longer rested on the bed. Maldito kept one hand wrapped firmly around Arturo's waist, and with the other he reached down and pulled Arturo's upper body off the bed and up against his body.

"Reach up with your Arms, Miho, and wrap your hands around my neck. Hold on tight."

Arturo did what he was told, and I saw the muscles of his arms kick in as he clasped his hands around Maldito's neck; Arturo's back was still pressed tightly against the huge man.

"Now hold on."

With uncanny strength Maldito moved to the edge of the bed and then stood up. He kept his hands wrapped around Arturo's body so that he would not fall.

They were now standing next to the chair I had been sitting in.

"Now, carefully place your feet on the chair."

Arturo did what he was told.

"Now let go and grab the back of the chair. Keep your knees bent. Don't worry, I won't let go of you and you won't tip over."

Arturo then grabbed the back of the chair and a soon as he did Maldito relaxed his grip around his chest.

"Now grab my cock, Miho, and guide it into you."

Arturo reached back with one hand and did not have to feel in the air for long before he found his uncle's cock. I saw that Arturo was once again looking in one of the mirrors as he pushed himself back against his 'uncle.'

It took a few seconds but Arturo let out a little yell when Maldito's cock head once again slipped in his hole. He quickly got over the initial pain of Maldito's cock once again being inside him, and slowly he bent at the knees and I saw the huge cock slowly disappear into Arturo's now insatiable hungry hole.

"Make your Papi proud, Miho. Show me how much you want it."

Arturo didn't waste any time before he was pushing up and down with his legs and over and over again began impaling his ass on the monster cock.

"Oh God, Papi, this feels so good!" yelled Arturo.

"I'm glad you like it, Miho, now hold the chair tightly. No One… " he said, looking over to me, "…come over here and brace the chair so that it does not tip over."

I quickly got up from the bed and went behind the chair so I was looking directly at Arturo in front of me who was still squatting and riding on his uncle's cock while standing on the chair.

"Hang on, Miho" Maldito exclaimed, when all of a sudden he reached down with both of his huge paws and grabbed Arturo under the inside of each of his legs and lifted him off the chair completely so that Arturo was now suspended, his hands holding the back of the chair and his uncle's cock still buried to the hilt in his ass.

"Now carefully put your hands on the seat of the chair, Miho."

I had to hold the chair in place as Arturo moved his hands down to the seat of the chair and kept them locked in place. He was now holding his upper body while his uncle had his ass impaled on his cock.

"Now hold on, Miho. I'm going to fuck you 'til I come."

With that, and still holding his nephew's hips easily in his hands, he began to push and pull Arturo's hole back and forth on his cock. Arturo started to grunt uncontrollably with each thrust, trying to hold onto the chair. I saw a look of determination come over Maldito's face as he pulled Arturo back and forth on his cock as if he as using Arturo's body as his own personal jackoff toy.

He continued to fuck him for a few more minutes, and I could tell that between getting a horse-sized cock jammed in and out of his ass and having to hold up his body with his arms, that Arturo was getting close to complete exhaustion.

All of a sudden Maldito was not only pulling Arturo's body back and forth but he also was forcing his cock up and in his adopted nephew's hole, each time sending Arturo's ass bouncing into the air. I watched as Arturo struggled to hang onto the chair.

"I'm cumming, Miho. Your Papi is fucking cumming in you, Miho!" He was almost yelling out the words and I expected someone to come into the room to see what the commotion was about, but no one came.

Maldito's thrusts were violent and finally Arturo's arms finally gave out and he fell forward. He should have fallen to the ground but he didn't as his uncle kept him impaled against him so hard that I thought Arturo's hips would surely break. Arturo looked like one of those cheap, plastic blow up dolls at this point, as Maldito clearly had no problem holding up his limp body as he continued his final spasms and shot his cum deep into Arturo's guts.

"Oh, fuck. Miho, that was good. I love you so fucking much, Miho." Maldito was beginning to relax his grip and as he did so I saw his cock pulling slowly out of Arturo's ass until the monster completely popped out and Arturo slowly slumped to the floor.

I was still standing behind the chair and I watched as Maldito straightened his back and brought his hands to his head and ran his fingers through his hair. I was almost in a trance as I saw his body now drenched in sweat. Even though I had cum a few minutes earlier I couldn't help but admire a man that even the most straight men in the world would no doubt be in awe of.

I looked down at Arturo who, now on the floor, had brought his knees into his chest and remained curled up, not moving. I could no longer see his ass but I knew that it had been punished more than most men would ever experience. I envied him a little but I also could see the look on his face that he clearly had been through something extremely traumatic as he continued to clasp his arms around his knees.

Maldito came to his senses much quicker than Arturo and I. He reached down and stripped the bed of its sheet. He then took it and quickly dried himself and wiped the lube off his cock and fingers.

He sat back down on the bed and without looking at me demanded, "Bring me my clothes, No One."

I did as he asked and carefully laid his clothes on the bed next to him and put his shoes and socks at his feet. I watched as he took his time getting dressed, careful to tuck in his shirt and put on his tie so that if anyone saw him they would not believe that he had just fucked the shit out of someone.

He got up and walked to one of the mirrors to inspect himself, reaching into his jacket pocket and pulling out his gloves and sunglasses and putting them on. He then turned around and walked back to where I stood, still naked.

"Now it's very important that you do as you are told, No One. You have pleased me more than I would have thought, and for that you should be very happy. But we are not done yet, and in fact the next few steps will be most important. I am going to leave this room and take care of this mess that Arturo has created. While I do, I want you to get dressed, and then get Arturo dressed. You will have no more than 5 minutes. Do you understand?"

"Yes, sir," I replied.

"Good. 5 minutes, No One. No more."

"We'll be ready, sir."

He reached over and grabbed his bag from the bed, walked to the door, and began to open it when he stopped and turned around.

"One more thing. I want you to call me Tio from now on. Tio means uncle if you did not know. This way I now have a new son and a new nephew to take his place. This is a very special day for me, indeed. Is that okay with you?"

I hesitated for just a second before responding, "Yes…Tio."

"I think we are going to get along just fine, No One." He smiled, then turned around, walked out the door, and closed the door behind him.

I stood there for few seconds and tried to get my mind around what had just happened. Although it had taken over 30 minutes it seemed like it had gone by in just seconds. I could still remember standing there as Maldito walked in the room, and now he was already gone.

I suddenly remembered what he had asked me to do and I quickly put on my own clothes. I then went over to where Arturo had not moved or said a word. I was worried that he had passed out but when I reached down to shake him he opened his eyes and looked at me.

"That was my father, and he forgives me." He said it in a way where I knew without a doubt that not only was he still as high as a kite, but thankfully he was not in a coma either. I was relieved.

"Come on, get up. You need to get dressed. Maldito needs us to get dressed. I think he wants us to leave with him."

Arturo first rolled to his knees and then with my help I grabbed him underneath his armpits and pulled him to his feet. He was in no way heavy but it reminded me how easily Maldito had held him in the air with apparent ease.

"Here, get your pants on. Here's your shirt."

I went around and grabbed his remaining clothes and watched as he slowly put them on. I had to help him with his shoes. He moved slowly, but he didn't appear to have any permanent damage. He didn't say a word as I helped him get dressed. I didn't have a watch but I knew that our 5 minutes was going to run out any second.

I had just finished lacing up his shoes when over the vibrating of the music in the other room I heard a Champaign cork pop. I didn't think anything of it other than maybe they were having some type of celebration. Then I heard another pop... and another... and another... and people began screaming.

I tugged on Arturo and got him to his feet, not knowing what to do, but being prepared for anything. I was getting ready to grab him and see if I could push him under the bed to hide, when the door opened and one of the two goons calmly walked in the room.

I stood there and waited to die.

"Come with me," he said. Looking at Arturo and seeing that he was not in a solid state of mind he added, "Bring him with you and make sure you do not let him go. Walk quickly. Let's go." He then walked out the door, leaving the door open behind him.

I walked slowly, wrapping my arm around Arturo's waist, and headed to the door and walked out into the hall. I didn't even have to exit the door before I saw the first body. It was a woman, and she was sprawled face down. There was a pool of blood spreading out on the side of her face that I could not see. I stopped momentarily before looking up and seeing the same goon motion with his hand, waving for me to keep up.

I don't know how I did it but somehow I did not collapse, although I could no longer feel my legs. I stepped forward, and over the woman, keeping hold of Arturo as I did. His head was down and although his legs were moving I doubt if he even knew what was going on.

As I walked down the hall, the doors to the once closed rooms were now open and I made the mistake of looking in one of them and saw two naked bodies covered in blood lying on the bed. I thought the man may have been Jake but I turned away quickly, afraid that I might vomit. My mind began shutting down in a defensive manner that I have never experienced before, but in a way that kept my focus on survival, and nothing more.

Although I saw several more bodies in the hallway, I did not stop and I did not let go of Arturo, holding him even tighter as if it was he who was holding me up instead of the other way around. As I entered the living room I did not stop as I saw several bodies on the couch and several others that looked as if they had tried to get out the front door before being shot. One of the men lying on the floor was Martin. I saw his dead eyes staring at the ceiling and I quickly turned away. As I stumbled to the door I was thinking that this hideaway apartment – a place that was a secret and designed to keep the world out – had turned out to be the same place that ended up becoming these people's tomb.

I eventually got to the door, practically dragging Arturo as he kept stepping on the bodies and tripping over them.

"Come on Arturo, we need to go. Please, Arturo, watch your step," I begged. I said these things as if I was instructing a child that it was time to leave the ice cream store and to watch out for any spilled ice cream as we did. But this was no spilled ice cream... these were dead bodies.

I finally got the both of us out the door and the fresh night air was intoxicating. I had also smelled things, nasty things, as I walked through the apartment but my brain did not process what they were until I once again had fresh air coursing through my lungs. I would never forget that smell of death for as long as I live.

I walked up the one level of stairs, dragging Arturo behind me and wondering why the goon ahead of me wasn't helping me. I looked up, getting ready to ask for help, and noticed that he was not focusing on us at all, but instead had his gun drawn and was carefully watching the surroundings with the calm intensity of a hawk looking for the wayward rabbit that would soon be his next meal. I changed my mind about asking him for help and instead just continued to drag Arturo up the steps.

When we got to the top of the stairs the largest four-door sedan I had ever seen pulled up as if the three of us had just robbed a bank and were waiting for the getaway car. Both of the side doors opened at once and I heard a voice instruct, "Put him in the back seat." The goon had already hopped in the front seat as I pulled Arturo over and practically tossed him into the open back seat door. I was ready to push him over when I saw a pair of large arms suddenly grab him from inside and pull him in. Not hesitating I hopped in the car and shut the door as the car was already pulling away.

I was out of breath from getting Arturo out of the apartment. I was looking around the interior of the car but the windows were tinted and it took me a second to adjust to what little light there was. I noticed that there was a window that stretched the width of the car, separating the front seats from the rear. I looked over and sitting next to me was Maldito, the man whose arms I had just seen. He was sitting up and had pulled Arturo close to him, with his arm around his shoulders holding him to his chest. I found myself leaning against the door as I looked over at the huge man who was now sitting next to me. I did not know what to say, so I said nothing.

"You did good, No One. Thank you," he said calmly.

My mind was still in shock and trying to block out the images that I just had seen, however it was failing as flashes of the people dead still ran through my mind. I tried to focus on what Maldito was saying but I heard the words as if they were coming from of a broken speaker system in another room.

"Is Arturo okay? " I asked quietly, noticing that Arturo had passed out completely. I wasn't sure if he was dead or alive.

Maldito looked down at the head of his adopted nephew as it rested on his chest. He reached up and with one hand stroked his shaved head.

"Arturo is fine. What we did may have been too much for him, but I think it's the drugs that have done him more harm. He will need to control his urges and I will discuss the problem with him when he awakens. But, how are you, No One? What is going through your mind, may I ask?"

He looked at me and I could see he was looking for some sign, some hint of what was truly going through my mind. There was a deep seriousness in his eyes that chilled the air between us. I felt as if he was looking to see if I could handle what I had just seen or whether I could not. I did not want to know what he would do if he felt that I could not hold on to what little sanity I still had left.

"I'm glad I'm out of there, and I have you to thank for it." I hesitated a few seconds as he continued to stare at me, looking for a glimpse of what truth I had behind my eyes that would give him what he needed to make any decision about my fate.

I continued.

"You saved me. I didn't want to be there anymore... thank you."

And I meant every word. I didn't care if he believed me or not. I didn't have anything left; I was emotionally raw and I couldn't have made something up if I tried. The only thing I could tell him was the truth and what would happen after that would just... happen.

He stared at me for what felt like minutes, but was no more than seconds. He then held out his upturned hand in a gesture that even in my current mental state told me he meant for me to take it, and I did. He easily covered my entire hand in his own as he closed his grip.

"Come closer," he said. I did as he asked and moved closer to him in the back seat. He released my hand but grabbed the upper part of my arm gently, making sure that he did not disturb Arturo. "Come closer so I can see your face. Do not be afraid of me, No One, I will not harm you. I did not expect that there would be a new Chico riding in this car today, but I find that I am glad there is."

Even sitting in the back of the large vehicle, he reminded me of a giant in a clown car. I leaned toward him, no longer afraid, as I did believe him when he said I nothing to fear. I got up on one knee so that I was only a foot from his face. He let go of my arm and moved it to the back of my neck, once again grasping me securely, but with a tenderness that one would not expect to see from such a man.

Slowly he leaned forward, and pulling my face to his he closed his eyes and brought his lips to mine, kissing me gently and holding them against his for a few, silent seconds. He pulled back, his lips falling away from mine. I watched as his eyes slowly opened, and he said in a whisper that I don't think even Arturo could have heard if he were awake:

"Welcome to the family, No One."

~oOo~

Within an hour I felt the car slow, and pull into what I presumed was a regional airport that I was not familiar with. The car pulled up to a jet and everyone quickly got out. I hesitated at first, and then slowly stepped out of the car also. I saw Maldito carrying Arturo up the steps and into the jet. I looked at the men surrounding me and they gave me no notice, instead taking several bags from the trunk and stowing them away in a compartment below the plane.

I walked over to the plane and slowly climbed the stairs. I looked back when I heard the car pull away and disappear into the darkness. I continued to climb the stairs and once at the top I hesitated for a second before lowering my head and entering the cabin.

When I climbed in I saw that Arturo had been placed in a chair that had been fully reclined. Maldito was sitting across from him. I looked at Maldito and he smiled again, holding out his arm, pointing to one of the chairs in front and across from him. I nodded, understanding, and walked over to the chair and slowly sat down. It was large and comfortable. I felt a humming noise and looked down and saw as Maldito pushed a lever on the side. I started to recline along with the chair and after a few seconds I relaxed. The chair stopped and I rolled my head to the side and looked over as Maldito once again returned to his chair.

I said nothing as several men, including the two goons that I had seen earlier, entered the plane. A man who I had not previously seen went to the front of the plane; the pilot, I figured. One of the other goons went as well and closed the curtain between the cabin and the cockpit. The other thug went to the back of the plane and sat down. He began to speak in Spanish to Maldito, but I did not understand. Considering what had just happened I was surprised at how calm they both were. They could have easily been discussing several rounds of golf they had just played.

I listened for a few minutes, the words getting lighter and softer as I closed my eyes. I felt the plane begin to shake slightly and I felt the familiar pull as the plane began to accelerate. With my eyes closed I felt the plane take off, gently but quickly. I opened my eyes and I saw that the fasten seat belt sign was on. I almost laughed, thinking that the only warning sign I had seen all day was one that told me to buckle my seat belt. I did as I was instructed and pulled the bands across my waist and pushed the two metal clasps together until they snapped. I pulled the strap hard, feeling the pressure as it held me in place. It felt oddly comforting.

I closed my eyes once again. I was calm, and didn't understand how that was possible. I pondered if I had lost something permanent, or if something was broken; something that was integral that allowed me to feel normal…to feel human. I wondered if I had lost part of my soul that evening and as I did I realized that I was no longer in the airplane at all. I had begun to dream. I dreamed of a tattooed god that was carrying me in his arms up to a heaven of white clouds that parted as he passed. He smiled down on me, a smile that told me that I was saved and that he was my savior. I closed my eyes in my dream and I slept – both in this world and the other.

~oOo~

I have been at the compound for 6 days. I have seen neither Maldito nor Arturo since arriving. There is a kitchen, and meals are made several times a day. I have not gone hungry. I am allowed to walk around freely, but it unnerves me as the men (and there are only men, no women) ignore me as if I wasn't there. They do not even look at me. Eventually I learned to ignore them as well as I explored the residence. It was small, but it was luxurious.

There was a much larger house on the cliffs above. I had seen several men walk the path that led upwards to the house. I expected that was where Maldito and Arturo were, but I was not certain. I did not try to go up the path myself. Something told me that if I tried I would find that the men would no longer ignore me.

So I wait. I wait for something that eludes me. And in this period of not knowing, I find a silence that forces me to think, but thinking has been very hard lately. I have closed the door and wept several times. I had not cried in years, and I do not understand why I cry.

Maybe by writing this down it will help, but I have no expectations at this point that anything will change. I can only blame myself… I think. But then I couldn't have expected anything like this and I find my tears changing from sadness to laugher. I feel crazy but I understand it at the same time. It's very confusing but when I look at myself in the mirror I still see myself, and not the stranger that my mind thinks I have become. It is something to hold onto, knowing that there may still be part of me inside that is hidden and afraid and waiting for the right time to come out and begin to put this life carefully back together again.

I'm going to put the pen down now as I feel tired. The beach looks nice, the sea calm, welcoming. But I am so tired. Maybe after I sleep I will be able to go outside and into the sun, and feel the sand and water on my feet as I walk along the beach.

Until then I will dream, and the man covered in tattoos will be there to comfort me.

Epilogue

Lieutenant Gaines slowly pulled into the parking lot. Most of the building has been sealed off with tape. He had driven around the front of the building and watched officers escorting the tenants out of the building and into the night air. He had instructed the officers to interview everyone to see if anyone had seen or heard anything in the previous hours. His instincts told him that they would get no leads. The call had come in only an hour earlier, but there were already over 10 patrol cars and several ambulances standing by. The media had gotten wind of the incident and he saw two officers watching them closely to make sure they didn't wander too far.

He had been through the drill before, but nothing of this magnitude. This was going to make the national news, and before he had left the house he had put on the one good jacket he owned, or at least the one that he knew he wife thought still made him look like the handsome policeman she had married 30 years earlier.

He knew how to deal with the press, and he knew that things were going to get very active over the next few days. He was retiring at the end of the year. He would not miss nights like this. The summer had been going so good until this night.

He parked on the far side of the lot and got out of the car. He spotted Detective O'Hara leaning down near what appeared to be a back entrance to the building. As he walked over to where the detective crouched, he looked at the surrounding buildings. There was no other building that was located right next to the apartment. It stood alone. He knew that unless someone had been watching the building that it would be doubtful anyone would have seen anything. He also understood that even if any neighbors had happened to be looking out their window, that they would most likely not want to talk to the cops. He didn't blame them. If this is what he thought it was, he wouldn't want to talk to the cops either. These folks weren't stupid.

Another officer was taking photographs of what appeared to be tire tracks, but Gaines doubted they would come up with anything. The men that did this would have made sure that nothing could be traced back to them. The work still had to be done though, and he made sure to walk a wide circle around the man trying to do his job at this late hour.

"Lieutenant," detective O'Hara called out.

"Detective," Gaines replied, as he walked up and shook the younger detective's hand.

"You put on your good suit. Your old lady sure knows how to make you look good when you need to."

"I wish I didn't have to. I received an initial report when I was driving over, but what have you got?"

"Twelve dead, no survivors. Looks like it was quick and efficient. This wasn't done by anyone in this neighborhood. This is something completely different. If I was to guess... and I'm not... I'd say this was the work of the Sinaloa cartel, but I've never seen anything like this."

"Hmm... maybe. Call up the DEA and bring them in. Until then, keep working the scene. What have you got out here?"

"Not much," the detective replied. "There are foot prints from the blood. They end right here where we've found some tire tracks. We're taking the pictures and we'll send them to the lab."

"Any drops of blood, or just foot prints?"

"No drops. Doesn't look like whoever did this was injured, although one of the prints looks as if the guy was limping, or being dragged. But no blood, so if he was hurt he wasn't bleeding."

"Sample everything to be sure. And the inside?"

"The place is clean. These folks didn't know what hit them. It doesn't look like they even had a chance to fight back. Each had at least two shots to the head. Whoever did this made sure that no one would be left to talk afterwards. We did find the same shoe prints on the floor inside the apartment, but as far as we can tell there isn't anything else. We've started looking for fingerprints but I got a feeling that we're not going to find anything. These guys knew exactly what they were doing and I doubt they would be so stupid as to pick up a glass with their bare hands."

"You're probably right. No one is perfect, though. They left something here, we just have to find it. So give me a breakdown on who has..."

A shout suddenly came from the bottom of the stairwell. "Lieutenant! Detective! You have to see this!" Gaines looked down and saw detective Carter waving them down.

"What have you found, detective?"

"You need to see this for yourself. I think we found the golden ticket!"

Both men began to walk down the stairs to where an excited detective Carter was standing, and continuing to talk quickly.

"We thought we had cleared the entire apartment but one of the men noticed that there was a crack in the bathroom wall that looked suspicious." He continued to talk as he entered the apartment and the two senior officers followed carefully behind. "Sure enough, we start to push on the wall and it moves. The fucking wall moved!"

"Language, detective."

"Shit, sorry sir. Well sure enough we pushed a little harder and the whole damn thing pushed back and there's another room back there. These fuckers were up to some freaky shit." Detective Carter glanced over his shoulder as he turned the hallway, "Sorry sir... language, I know."

"Who's been in there?" asked detective O'Hara.

"The hidden room? No one. We just found it a few minutes ago."

"Show me," asked the Lieutenant.

Detective Carter walked down the hallway, leading the way, and Gaines looked around the apartment as he followed. It was a massacre all right. Not a table overturned, or even a plate on the floor. These poor people went down, and down fast.

"Right here, Lieutenant," Detective Carter motioned, pointing to the bathroom that was located right before the end of the hallway and on the right. "Take a look."

Gaines walked past the other officer and into the bathroom. No one had been in the bathroom apparently when the shootings took place. If they had, there would have been a dead body on the floor. Across from the toilette was a small hole in the wall, perfectly square, that was no more than three feet high and three feet across. He pulled out his flashlight, turned it on, and bent down on one knee and looked inside.

"What do you see, Lieutenant?" asked O'Hara.

Gaines lowered himself as close to the floor as possible and peered into the room. Without getting up or turning to look at the other officers he said, "Turn on the light in the room at the end of the hall."

"What for, Lieutenant? Did you see it? You see it, don't you?" asked Carter.

"Just do it."

Detective Carter didn't hesitate and walked out of the bathroom and to the room located next door. He flipped on the light to the bedroom and went back to the bathroom. "Lights on, Lieutenant."

Gaines stayed on the floor and the two officers watched as he peered into the hidden room, shining his flashlight into all corners. He stayed on the ground for several minutes before slowly getting up.

"So did you see, Lieutenant? Did you see it?" asked Carter.

"Yes, I saw it."

"Goddamn, I told you we found the golden ticket!" exclaimed Carter.

"What's in there, chief?" asked O'Hara.

Gaines didn't say anything for several seconds. He looked at the wall of the bathroom and slowly walked into the hallway and looked into the room located next door. He saw the mirrors, saw the bed, and the rumpled sheets tossed on the floor. He noticed that unlike the other two bedrooms, there were no bodies in this room. There were no bloody foot prints either.

He turned right and walked halfway to the corner and stopped. He squatted down again and pulled out his flashlight, and pointed it directly at the mirror.

"What you got, Lieutenant?" asked "O'Hara.

"It's a mirror."

"I see that. But what are you looking at?"

"It's a two-way mirror."

"And...?"

"And there is a video camera on the other side in the hidden room."

Detective O'Hara stared at the lieutenant for a few seconds before responding, "So, you think..?"

"Yes. Whoever was in this room may be on that video camera... and I don't think they knew it." Gaines stood up and walked to the bedroom door, looking at the floor as he did. "There's no bodies in here. Why? I'm guessing that's because whoever killed these people were in this very room and they walked right out of here. The footprints begin right outside this door and they go all the way through the apartment and outside."

Gaines looked at O'Hara before continuing. "Let's see what's on that camera."

"Damn, Lieutenant. So we got 'em. We got the motherfuckers!" exclaimed detective Carter.

"Yes, detective, I think we do... and watch the language."

The End

Here is a sample from another story you may enjoy:

JACOB SLATER

WILD AFTERNOON DELIGHT

The Zone Series, Book 1

GAY EROTICA

First, my name is Adam. I am about 5'8", 155 lbs., toned, smooth and muscular. People tell me that I look a lot like a blonde version of Zach Efron, although I think I'm better looking and not such a dork. I am athletic, but also a self-described preppy, but not in a nerdy way. I come from an affluent background. My father does quite well financially and we live in a fairly prestigious neighborhood of Chicago. I was into all sorts of sports in high school including football, soccer, wrestling, and baseball. As I indicated, I just graduated from high school this past spring. I'm 18 years old.

In terms of my personal life, I've had many, many girlfriends but I don't have one currently. I've found that finding girls is quite easy, but once you have one and they claim you as their own, they can turn into quite the pain in the ass. I know one day I'll have to think about getting into a serious relationship, but not now; not the summer before I head off to college.

I have many friends, mostly guys who are a lot like me: popular, good-looking, jocks. Although I have many friends, I can't say I have that one best friend that I can share everything and anything with. They'll tell me about the girls they've been with, the wild parties they went to, etc. I even have a buddy who tells me how often he beats off and the girls he wishes he were fucking. I think he wants me to share some of the same things with him, but I don't. I just listen and laugh, but rarely share any of my inner thoughts or secrets. Maybe that is why I'm struggling now with what happened; I just don't have anyone to talk to.

Although I had a couple of buddies call up and ask me to hang out with them last Friday afternoon I decided that I needed some 'me' time, and like I have done many times before I decided I just wanted to get out of the house and take a walk. I told my mother I was heading out, and I honestly told her, when she asked where I was going, that I was just taking a walk down to the lake. She knew I liked to get out and just walk. And although she always seemed to worry about me, she never discouraged me when I just wanted to get out and get some fresh air. I had never gotten into any serious trouble and she had no reason to think today would be any different; neither did I, for that matter.

It was around 4:00 in the afternoon and I was walking down Lake Shore Drive. It was in the middle of summer and I had on a pair baggy shorts and a tee shirt that I had draped over my shoulder. I was thinking about why I didn't spend more time with my friends lately and why I preferred to spend so much time alone. I briefly wondered if there was something wrong with me, but I knew that wasn't the case and pushed those thoughts out of my head. There was something missing in my life, I knew that, but I couldn't quite figure out exactly what it was. I knew enough to know that many teenagers struggled to find their identity, especially at my age, and most likely I was just going through that period in my adolescence when I had to discover who I was, and the man that I wanted to become. College was the next major step in my life and I felt comforted knowing that maybe that was why I was feeling anxious as of late.

I had been walking for about an hour when I felt the urge to take a leak. There are many restrooms scattered along the lake in the northern part of Chicago, and looking around I saw one that was located next to one of the many parking areas. When I entered the bathroom I noticed one other man who was already standing at the urinal taking a leak. He was black, in mid 40s or so, and was very tall, at about 6'4" or possibly a little taller, as it was dark in the restroom. Even though I was in a public restroom I briefly hesitated walking further into the room, as the man was quite a bit larger than myself and something about him gave me reason to pause, but I couldn't explain why. I only hesitated a couple of seconds though, and then brushing off any concerns, I walked up to the only other urinal in the restroom and started to take a piss. I wasn't pissing for 5 seconds when the man began to talk to me.

"What's up today, boy? What you doing out here at the lake today?" he asked.

I was surprised that he began a conversation with me. I briefly wondered if I should have followed my earlier instincts when I first entered the restroom. "I'm just getting out of the house. Bored, you know?" I answered, glancing at him nervously, before once again looking down at myself as I tried to continue to piss, which was getting more difficult by the second.

I could see that he was continuing to stare at me. "So you just hangin'?" he asked.

"Yeah," I replied and looked at him again. I was now aware that he was no longer peeing and was just holding his dick. Trying not to look like I was staring, but out of the corner of my eye, I could see that he was holding his cock and shaking it a little. I couldn't believe that this guy was actually checking me out. This was not the first time this had happened. I knew that some of these bathrooms were cruised by men looking for sex. I had been cruised before and it was easy enough to blow guys off and just walk out, problem solved. For reasons I cannot understand even now, I did not leave and I remained in place.

I felt awkward just standing there, and the silence between the two of us was getting more uncomfortable by the second. I was no longer pissing into the urinal and normally I would have zipped up and walked out. But something about the combination of nervousness and curiosity kept my feet locked in place. As the silence between the two of us continued I realized that both of us had quit pissing. We were both still just standing there, cocks in our hands.

I couldn't handle the silence any longer. "So, what are you up to?" I found myself asking, still staring ahead but glancing out of the side of my eyes at the big man standing next to me.

Continuing to hold his cock, he turned towards me, tilted his head to the side a little, and replied "Just looking to have some fun, if you know what I mean." He then really started to wag his cock at me, which by now I was looking at directly and could see that it was very, very fat. I couldn't really tell how long it was because he was wearing baggy jeans, but I knew it was a lot bigger than mine and a hell of a lot bigger than the few friends and classmates that I had seen in the showers at school.

All my instincts told me to get the hell out of there. Here was a guy more than twice my age, and about twice my size, coming right out and letting me know that he wanted to have some 'fun' with me; whatever that meant. I didn't have any attraction to this guy, or any guys for that matter. I just didn't do those types of things with guys. Plus, he was disgusting anyway. But still, I didn't move and after a few seconds the man came closer and cupped my ass with his other hand. I was startled and jumped a little, but the guy kept his hands on my butt. I remember thinking that he had big hands when he surprised me once again when he squeezed my ass and I felt his fingers dig deep into my skin.

"You gotta nice ass there, boy. You must like this because you ain't gone anywhere yet. How about we get outta here and go back to my place. It's not very far. We'll be there in 5 minutes. How 'bout it?"

Although it's hard for me to write this now, even to myself, I have often wondered about my sexuality. I knew I liked girls and I easily lost my virginity a couple of years ago. I had let many girls suck my dick as many of them preferred to do that when they didn't want to get fucked. I have cum many times with girls so I knew I didn't have any performance issues. I generally liked sex with girls, I really did... but each time I went home I wondered what it would have been like if it had been with a guy instead of a girl. I'd never done anything with a guy, but I can't lie to myself any longer that the idea of it had been with me for quite some time. Maybe that was why there were times when I just wanted to take a walk by myself; hoping that maybe I can try and make sense of it all.

So yeah, I admit it. I have often fantasized about what my first sexual experience with a guy would be like and I was beginning to get more comfortable with the idea that maybe it was time for me to be more honest with myself, and stop fighting those urges. But I can guarantee you that standing there in that bathroom, and looking over at this big, black man, that I didn't think this would be that first experience. However, there was something about the demanding look that the man was giving me. He somehow knew he was in control of the situation and he knew it. He could tell that I was a little scared, but he obviously could also tell I was curious and interested. He was clearly reading me faster than I was reading him.

It must have been the look on my face because he simply said, "Let's go," and he zipped up his pants and headed out of the bathroom toward the parking lot. For a few seconds I thought about the situation I found myself in, and ignoring every fiber of my being I followed after him.

Neither one of us said anything as we walked. I stayed a little bit behind him so it wouldn't look as if we were actually together. He walked up to a small, cheap car and got in. He then reached over and unlocked the passenger side door. As soon as I got in the car and closed the door I noticed the smell of cigarettes. No sooner did I notice, he reached in his pocket and lit one up. I hated cigarettes and hated the smell especially, but I didn't say anything. He put the car in gear and we pulled away from the parking lot with him giving me a quick glance. When he looked at me he had a smirk on his face as if something was amusing him.

"Is something wrong?" I asked, wondering and slightly hoping that maybe the man was changing his mind.

If you enjoyed this sample then look for <u>Wild Afternoon Delight.</u>

If you enjoyed any of my books then please share the love and click like on my books in Amazon.

If you write me a review and send me an email I will send you a free book, or many.
(Just know that these emails are filtered by my publisher.)

Good news is always welcome.

One Last Thing, For Kindle Readers...

When you turn the page, Kindle will give you the opportunity to rate this book and share your thoughts on Facebook and Twitter. If you enjoyed my writings, would you please take a few seconds to let your friends know about it? Because... when they enjoy they will be grateful to you and so will I.

Thank You!

Jacob Slater
jacob_slater@awesomeauthors.org